"Where in holy hell have you been?"

Wade was angry, dangerously angry, but Samantha refused to cower. She stuck her hands on her hips and her chin in the air. "I was working on the case."

"Alone." He grabbed her shoulders. "I told you not to go without me."

Sam stood her ground. "You didn't show."

"I was late, damn it. Do you know how many times I tried to reach you? Do you have any idea how worried I've been?"

Puzzled, she stared at him. His face was a mask of fury and frustration. "Why?"

He looked at her as if she'd lost her mind. "Why?" He let out a ragged breath. "Because I want you safe. I want you in one piece." His hands gentled on her shoulders. "Damn it, Sam, I just want you...."

Lorna Michaels's husband grows peppers, uses them to cook dishes that can scorch your insides and recommends them for everything from malaise to migraines. When Lorna tagged along with him to sample the offerings at a chili cook-off, she got the idea for *The Great Chili Caper*. Her research led them to Terlingua during the International Chili Championship, an unforgettable experience. Cindy Reed, whose recipe is included here, was the first-place winner at Terlingua in 1992 and 1993. Write to Lorna and Cindy at P.O. Box 31400, Houston, TX 77235-1400.

Books by Lorna Michaels

THE GREAT CHILI CAPER
Lorna Michaels

Harlequin Books

TORONTO • NEW YORK • LONDON
AMSTERDAM • PARIS • SYDNEY • HAMBURG
STOCKHOLM • ATHENS • TOKYO • MILAN
MADRID • WARSAW • BUDAPEST • AUCKLAND

To my husband, Ralph,
who promised if I went to a chili cook-off with him,
I'd get a book out of it.

And special thanks to Shannon Donahue
for help with an important scene.

ISBN 0-373-25684-1

THE GREAT CHILI CAPER

Copyright © 1996 by Thelma Zirkelbach.

Bobby Ray Shelton's country-western bar reeked of cigarette smoke, beer and cheap perfume, just the way Nick Petrelli liked it. He propped a booted foot on the rung of the next stool, took a swig from a cool Lone Star and scanned the room. He'd driven in from the ranch to meet a fellow named Al McGuire, and he wondered what was taking the guy so long.

The door opened and a high-class babe walked in, looking as out of place in Bobby Ray's as a flea at the fancy Westminster Dog Show. She gave the place a once-over, sashayed up to the bar and took the stool next to Nick.

WADE PHILLIPS scowled at the computer on his desk, battling an urge to kick a hole through the screen with his boot. Three hours sitting on his butt in front of the keyboard and this was all he had to show for it. Two lousy paragraphs. And his publisher expected the book in less than two months. Hell, he didn't even know who the fancy broad who'd flounced into Bobby Ray's was or why she'd planted herself next to Nick. The curse Wade uttered would have shocked even Nick Petrelli, and not much on this earth could shock the tough cowboy-detective of Wade's fabulously successful mystery series.

If he didn't get this book to his publisher by his deadline— one that his editor caustically reminded him had been extended twice—Wade *and* Nick would be dead in the water.

Trouble was, Wade based Nick's exploits on his own cases as a private investigator, and not one case of more than passing interest had crossed his desk at Phillips Investigations in the past six months. Stolen jewelry—Nick had dealt with that in book number three. Murder—books two and five.

"Make something up," his agent had bellowed, but Wade stood firm. Wade might embellish or modify them, but Nick Petrelli's cases were authentic ones from the files of a real private eye, and that wasn't going to change.

The telephone rang.

Wade considered ignoring it. The caller probably wanted to sell him aluminum siding or a magazine subscription. On the other hand...

"Phillips Investigations."

"Mr. Phillips?" The female voice was sultry.

"Yeah."

"This is Samantha Brewster. I'm calling for my grandfather, Clint Brewster. I suppose you've heard of him."

The chili czar. "Hasn't everyone?"

"He wants to see you."

Interesting. Wade tucked the receiver under his jaw and grabbed a pencil. "Why?"

"Some company documents are missing."

"What kind of documents?" Wade asked.

"He'd rather explain that in person. Could you meet with him this afternoon at two o'clock?"

Wade glanced at his bare appointment book. "I'll...work him in." Let Brewster think he was busy. In fact, his only current job was tailing an executive with a yen for women younger and more energetic than his wife. The fellow didn't let his extracurricular activities interfere with his work schedule, so Wade wouldn't be busy until evening. He took down Brewster's address, not surprised that he lived in one of Houston's most affluent suburbs.

He broke the connection and looked up as the office door opened. Carla Burns, his chronically late secretary, strolled in. Wade glanced pointedly at his watch.

Carla shrugged and emptied a plastic bag containing three bottles of nail polish in assorted colors, a crossword-puzzle book and a copy of *How to Survive Your Child's Teenage Years* on her desk. "Sorry. The orthodontist ran late, and then I had to drop Kim off at school. I didn't think you'd mind. We're not exactly overrun with work here."

Wade waved the slip with Brewster's address. "We are now."

"A call?"

"Yep. From Clint Brewster."

"Wow! Mr. Chili himself." Carla sat at her desk and fluffed her auburn hair. "What'd he want?"

"To meet with me this afternoon about some documents missing from his company."

Carla grinned. "A new job!"

"Yeah, and hopefully one that'll help Nick out. We'll see." Wade leaned back, put his feet on the desk and sighed deeply. "I should have let the mob kill Nick off when they kidnapped him in the last book."

"And leave your readers in limbo? You've got more books in you."

"Maybe they're somewhere, but they're sure not coming out," Wade muttered, raking his fingers through his hair.

"They will. Cheer up, Wade. No one ever died of writer's block."

Wade wasn't so sure. At any rate, he had an excuse to forget about Nick for a while as he ran a background check on Clint Brewster. He believed in meeting new clients armed with as much information on them as possible. Wade had to check out his potential-client-to-be before two o'clock. He began with a call to his contact at the Houston *Express*. "See what you can dig up on Clint Brewster." While he waited, he logged on to the Internet.

Everyone knew that ol' Clint had begun as a roughneck in the East Texas oil fields. He'd carried lunches of his mother's chili to work and word had gotten around the oil patch that Hilda Brewster's chili was delicious. Soon Clint had given up roughnecking and had started peddling chili. From that inauspicious beginning, Down Home Foods had grown into a company with an impressive array of products. From an article archived under misc.entrepreneur, Wade learned that at seventy-two, Clint Brewster still ruled with an iron hand the company he'd begun fifty years ago.

Biographical information from the data base told him Clint had been married to his wife, Martha, for forty-seven years, had fathered two sons and a daughter. Wade's buddy at the *Express* contributed details from a recent feature on the food magnate, indicating that Clint was in top physical shape. He swam laps in his pool each morning, played golf and tennis, and recently had participated in an Outward Bound trek for seniors.

Clint Brewster was renowned not only for his business success, Wade learned, but also for his philanthropy. His Brewster Foundation funded a home for teenage boys, research in cystic fibrosis—a grandson had died of the disease—and a Texana collection at a local museum.

Wade took a break from the background check to grab a sandwich from the deli downstairs. When he returned to his office and opened the door, he heard Carla's voice. "Yes, Harold, I think Nick's back in business. I'll tell Wade you called—oh, here he is now."

Wade scowled at Carla as he headed for the phone. She'd been talking to his agent, Harold Borden. Harold had been calling from New York almost daily to check on the progress of his star client.

Damn! Carla, who had a talent for overstepping her bounds, had really jumped the gun this time. Harold didn't need to know about the new job until Wade had had a chance to decide if he wanted it. Too late now. Sighing in resignation, he picked up the receiver. "Yeah, Harold."

"So!" Harold's voice, classic Brooklyn and gravelly from forty years of smoking, blasted Wade's eardrum. "Nick's got a job."

"*I've* got a job . . . maybe."

Harold ignored the maybe. One of the toughest and most successful literary agents in the business, he didn't deal in maybes. "Industrial espionage," he said. "That's a new one. Thank God!"

"Wait a minute, Harold. I haven't—"

"I'm putting in a call to Francine."

"No! Don't call my editor. Harold! Harold? Damn!" Wade slammed down the receiver. "He hung up." He swung around to face Carla. "Why'd you tell him?" he snarled.

"He asked me." Looking unconcerned, Carla stapled several papers and slid them into a manila folder.

"He *asked* me," Wade mimicked. "Ever hear of lying?"

"Nick never lies."

Wade dropped his head into his hands and counted to ten. "Carla," he said, "Nick is not real."

"Millions of readers think he is."

Wade couldn't argue with that, or with the fact that those readers had made him a rich man. And if the good Lord was willing and Clint Brewster had a hot case for him, Wade would give his readers what they craved—another opportunity to follow the twists and turns of a private investigation, Nick Petrelli style.

AN HOUR LATER, as he negotiated Houston's freeway system on the way to Clint Brewster's Memorial-area address, Wade pondered the role of the fictional Al McGuire in paragraph one of Nick's new saga. A company official? Too tame. A corporate spy? Better. He'd heard that with government spying on the wane, ex-agents were hiring out to private industry.

Wade turned down the driveway into the Brewster estate and lost his train of thought. The house looked like something straight out of *Gone With the Wind*. White, three-storied, with graceful columns along a wide veranda. A wide blue door. Trees and flowers in lush profusion. When he crossed the porch and rang the bell, he fully expected a character from Margaret Mitchell's novel to answer the door.

Instead, a small, gray-haired man with half glasses perched on a sharp nose pulled open the door. "Yes, sir?"

"Wade Phillips. I'm here to see Mr. Brewster."

"I'll tell him you're here."

"No need, Harrison. I'll take him up."

The voice came from the stairway. Because the stairs curved to the side, Wade couldn't see the speaker, but he recognized the voice. The woman who'd called him this morning.

He waited, watching as white sandals appeared on the steps, then long slim legs encased in a pair of wheat-colored linen shorts. Man, what legs! Then he forgot the legs as the rest of her came into view. She was wearing a loose-fitting white blouse in some filmy material that provided a tantalizing hint of what lay beneath. Wade couldn't see, but he could damn sure imagine.

Another step down and he saw her face. Summer-blond hair pulled back and secured with a clip. High cheekbones. Soft lips tinted a pale coral. She looked like a princess—cool, regal, untouchable. Then she came closer and he met her eyes. Large, thickly lashed and anything but cold, they were the color of whiskey and packed the same punch. He thought of sizzling sexuality beneath an ice-cool surface. Keeping his mind on business this afternoon would be tough.

She extended her hand. "Mr. Phillips."

"Ms. Brewster." Her hand was slender, fine-boned, but surprisingly strong.

"If you'll follow me . . ."

Baby, I'd follow you anywhere. He climbed the stairs behind her, appreciating a back view almost as enticing as the front.

One flight up, she motioned him down a richly carpeted hall. Impressionist prints hung on the walls—fuzzy shapes in vibrant colors. At the end of the hallway, she stopped, tapped on a door and pushed it open. Wade followed her inside a large, wide-windowed study and had his first view of Clint Brewster. Of course, he'd seen pictures of him in the newspaper, but in person the man surpassed his photos.

The chili czar had steel-gray hair and piercing blue eyes that Wade sensed were sizing him up. He was casually dressed in dark blue pants and a white sport shirt open at the neck. Unlike many wealthy men Wade had met, Clint wore no jewelry except the plain gold watch at his wrist. He wasn't a big man, but he gave the impression of being larger than life. *The look of a legend.*

Brewster walked over to him, shook Wade's hand and motioned him to a chair. "Glad you could come out on such short notice."

"No problem." Wade sat down.

Samantha took the chair beside his and kicked off her shoes, then curled up like a sleek cat.

Clint gestured to a well-stocked bar in one corner of the room. "Would you like a drink?"

"No, thanks. I never drink on the job." The last time he had, the job had ended in disaster and he wasn't about to take a chance on that happening again. Besides, he thought bourbon tasted like antifreeze, and his contact at the *Express* had told him that Clint drank nothing else.

Clint went to the bar and returned with a glass filled with amber liquid. He sat down and took a long swallow. "I've been asking around for a private investigator. Everywhere I checked, your name came up. They say you're good. Are you?"

Wade grinned. "The best."

"That's what I need." Clint leaned forward. "I've got a problem, Phillips. A big one." He hesitated a moment. "This is confidential, of course."

"Of course."

For a moment, Clint stared out the window at the wide expanse of lawn below them, then he said, "We're about to introduce a new chili. Hottest one we've ever made. Market studies say the public's ready for a spicier taste."

Lord, Wade thought. *Do they have to do market studies on chili?*

"Naturally," Clint continued, "the recipe's a closely guarded secret."

"Naturally."

"Not so secret anymore." Clint's voice turned cold. "Someone stole it." He slammed his fist on the massive mahogany desk. Beside Wade, Samantha jumped. "I filled in for a friend and judged a chili cook-off a couple of weeks ago. One of the recipes tasted familiar."

"You could tell from a taste?"

"Young man, I can recognize my recipes from the smell. What I tasted was mine, without a doubt."

"Did you check to see if the recipe was missing?"

"We keep our recipes in a protected computer file with limited access. It was there, of course, but sure as I'm sitting here, someone got to that file and made a copy."

"Who entered it in the cook-off?" Wade asked.

"Two guys who called themselves the Hot Hombres. I went to the cook-off organizers and got a copy of their registration." He tossed a sheet of paper across the desk.

"Don and Dale Barkley," Wade read.

"I checked them out. The names are phony. So's the address," Clint said with disgust. "That's when I decided I needed a detective."

"Could these guys have broken into your computer file?" Clint shook his head. "Or had a contact in your company who could?"

"Only a few people have access to that file," Clint said. "I'd trust any of them with my life."

Wade wouldn't, but then, he'd seen the seamy side of life too much to trust anyone with his. "Someone else might've set up those fellows to test out the recipe," he said, thinking aloud. "Who'd want it?"

"Plenty of people," Samantha said. "Hundreds."

"Try to narrow the field."

Clint pushed a list across the desk. "Here are a few possibilities." He sighed. "When you're on top, everyone is out to knock you down."

Wade glanced at the paper. "These people are your competitors, right?" When Clint nodded, Wade said, "How about the names of the people inside the company? The ones with access to the file. Or someone who doesn't have access but knows about the product." Clint took back the paper and scribbled some names.

"Okay, now disgruntled employees, someone who's been fired maybe," Wade suggested.

"I'll have to give that some thought," Clint said. Then he leaned forward. "If word of the theft gets out, do you have any idea what it could do to Down Home Foods? It would murder our reputation, send our stock plummeting. I'm in the midst of delicate negotiations for a merger with K and M

Frozen Foods, but we've got tough competition. K and M's flirting with two other companies, outfits that would do anything to undermine Down Home Foods to get what they want. I can't risk anyone finding out, understand?"

Wade nodded.

"So," Clint said, "tell me how you run your investigations."

Wade went over his standard operating procedure.

Clint nodded as he listened. "You interested in taking this case?"

"Yes, sir." He was interested for himself and also for Nick. Besides, he thought, glancing at Samantha out of the corner of his eye, he could imagine an added benefit. Taking this case might give him a chance to get to know the luscious lady better. He went over his usual charges with Clint, they signed the standard agreement Wade had brought with him, then he pointed to the list Clint had handed him earlier. "Give me a rundown on your relationship with these people."

Clint rose. "Samantha will do that. My wife, Martha, and I are leaving for London in an hour. Be gone two weeks. Anyway, Sam will be working with you."

"I beg your pardon?"

Clint, halfway to the door now, glanced over his shoulder. "My granddaughter here has a yen to be a private eye. You and she will be working together." He walked out and shut the door.

Wade stared dumbfounded at Samantha Brewster.

Looking unperturbed, she stared back.

"Did I hear him right?" Wade muttered.

"You certainly did."

For a moment, he was too furious to respond. Then he snarled, "I work alone."

"Not this time."

Be careful what you wish for. You might get it. Not two minutes ago, he'd told himself he would like to get to know Samantha Brewster better, but he sure hadn't meant as a colleague. He'd taken on an inexperienced partner once before and lost him in a set-up drug buy that had gone awry. He didn't want to risk that happening again. *Damn!* If he had any choice in the matter, he would take that signed contract, tear it to shreds and scatter it on the plush carpet beneath his feet.

But he had no choice. He needed the case. *Nick* needed the case. People were counting on him—his agent, his editor, his fans. "Look," he said, controlling his temper with an effort, "be reasonable. This is a high-stakes case, the kind that requires someone with experience."

"I have experience," she said, her tone implacable.

"What kind?"

"I worked with a private investigator in Dallas."

"Doing what?" He looked her up and down. *Modeling clothes for the fashionable P.I.?*

Samantha tossed her head. "I'm a photographer. He needed some specialized work on a case. I did a good job so he gave me more work, and I got interested."

Wade couldn't help it. He burst out laughing. "And you think that qualifies you to work as an investigator?"

"I think—"

"Look, doll, you want to play Nancy Drew, fine. But not on my time."

Her eyes heated. "*Our* time, Mr. Phillips. And don't call me doll."

"No? You want me to call you *Miz* Brewster?" he asked with all the insolence he could muster.

"Try Sam. That's my name."

"Oh, baby." His gaze raked over her. "I could never think of you as Sam."

"Work at it," she said, standing up and motioning toward the door. He began to stalk out. As he passed her, she said coolly, "I don't answer to baby, either."

Frustrated, he marched past her and turned down the hall. On the way downstairs, with Sam following, he told himself he'd give her some glorified busywork, keep her happy and out of his hair. Yeah, that would do the trick. In no time at all she'd be bored out of her mind and hooked on some other career—belly dancing or marine biology. In fact, he had a little job for her right off the bat.

Wade opened the front door and they stepped out on the veranda. He smiled at her and held out the paper Clint had given him. "Look, d—, uh, Sam, why don't you take this list of names and write down the connection each one of them has to your grandfather. We'll get together and go over it."

"Fine. When?"

Mentally, he reviewed his schedule. Tail the CEO tonight, write chapter one tomorrow, maybe chapter two. "How about tomorrow evening?"

"Sure. I'm staying in Granddad's guest house. It's just down the driveway," she said, waving her hand in the appropriate direction. "Nine o'clock."

Abruptly, they both turned as a red Jaguar roared down the driveway and screeched to a stop. A slender brunette dressed in navy shorts and one of the tightest T-shirts Wade had ever seen emerged and headed in their direction. "Hey, Sam, ready to go?" she asked as she crossed the porch.

"In a minute. Tonya, this is Wade Phillips. My cousin, Tonya Brewster."

Tonya examined him thoroughly, then she smiled appreciatively. "Very nice . . . to meet you, Wade. Are you a friend of Sam's?"

Before he could answer, Samantha said airily, "Wade does investigative work. Granddad just hired him to help me locate some documents."

Wade's mouth fell open. Help *her!* As Samantha gave him a triumphant smile, he muttered so only she could hear, "Your point, *doll.*" Then, with a nod to both women, he strolled off.

Sam and Tonya watched as Wade ambled down the driveway. "Nice build," Tonya said.

"Mmm."

"Interesting face, too. You should photograph him, Sam, start a rogues' gallery. He could be your star rogue. He has that look—dark and dangerous."

"Really?"

"Come on." Tonya laughed. "Don't tell me you didn't see, Ms. Photographer. Those glorious blue eyes, that sexy grin, those cute buns. And that swagger as he walked away. You'd have to be dead not to notice."

"I noticed."

"Good, you're still alive. What's he really doing here?" she asked as they walked toward the Jaguar.

"Just what I said. He's the private investigator Granddad hired to find the missing recipe."

"Ah," Tonya said. "He looks the type. A little on the shady side. Like I said, dark and dangerous."

Sam got into the car and slammed the door. "Don't romanticize him. Being a detective is just a job."

Tonya started the engine. "Maybe, but don't tell me he doesn't turn you on." When Samantha said nothing, Tonya added, "Just a little?"

"Okay, just a little. A minuscule amount." *Well, maybe not so minuscule*, she admitted to herself. Wade Phillips was vaguely menacing, in an intriguing way. All right, a very intriguing way.

"And you're going to be working together," Tonya continued. "Did you find out if he's single?"

"Divorced."

"Good. You came right out and asked him, hmm?"

Sam grimaced. "Of course not. I had my P.I. friend in Dallas check him out. He included that information in the file."

"Well, you two should have an interesting relationship." Samantha let that pass, and Tonya grinned at her. "So, where to first, Nancy Drew?"

"Neiman Marcus," Samantha said. "And don't call me Nancy Drew."

"Oh, loosen up, Sam. Stop being so defensive." Tonya gave her a knowing glance. "What's wrong? Have your parents been reading you the riot act about going into private investigating?"

Sam sighed. "Mother spent so long on the phone haranguing me, my ear went numb." She mimicked her mother's voice. "Private investigating is not an appropriate career choice for the post-debutante daughter of Camilla Brewster. And what's more, it's dangerous."

"Well, she's right on both counts."

Sam muttered something unprintable.

"Let me see," her cousin said as she floored the gas pedal and swerved around a delivery van, "an appropriate career choice for you would be . . . a tour guide in a museum."

Sam snorted.

"Or the headmistress of an exclusive girls' prep school."

"Mother would rather I didn't work at all. She'd like to

marry me off to a suitable millionaire and watch me spend the rest of my life sipping tea at the Junior League."

"That'll be the day. On the other hand, I'm sure Grand-daddy supports you in your current venture." Sam nodded, and Tonya continued, "You've always been his favorite. I should be jealous, but you know what, cuz? I'm not."

"Thanks."

Tonya shot through a yellow light, careened around a corner and kept going. "But seriously, Sam," she added, "your parents have good reason to worry about your safety."

"How well I know." She and her younger sister, Susan, had been kidnapped when they were eleven and eight. Sam had escaped, but Susan had been held hostage for nearly two weeks. Since then, her parents had been almost paranoid in their concern for their daughters. Only Sam's own strength and willpower had prevailed against them and allowed her to lead a normal life. "You know, the police did a rotten job of handling the kidnapping," she mused aloud. "If we hadn't hired a private detective, we would never have gotten Susan back."

Tonya grinned. "Hence, Samantha Spade, private eye."

"Right. And what career have you chosen, cousin dear?"

Tonya tossed her long brown hair. "Me? I'm planning to run away and join the circus."

WADE FLIPPED ON his computer. He'd pushed aside his anger about having Samantha as a collaborator and focused on his book. Ideas had buzzed in his head all the way back to the office. He'd change the chili company to pet food, Clint Brewster would be an aristocratic Virginian, and now he knew who Al McGuire was. He called up the appropriate file and reread the last line:

She gave the place a once-over, sashayed up to the bar and took the stool next to Nick.

He continued typing.

"Nick Petrelli?" she said.

"Yeah."

She reached into the pocket of silk pants so tight he could see the outline of a mole on her backside, pulled out a card and slapped it on the bar beside him. "I'm Al."

Nick choked on his beer.

2

WADE PARKED in the driveway of the Brewster estate, got out of his car and meandered toward the guest house, enjoying the balmy September evening. No need to hurry. He'd arrived twenty minutes early.

He passed a graceful gazebo, then approached the small house. Tall pines and spreading oak trees, their limbs dripping with moss, surrounded it. Like the main residence, this one was white brick. French doors opened onto a back patio furnished with white wrought-iron tables and chairs. Wade turned and walked along the side of the house, glancing through long windows into the lighted living room.

Samantha had company.

The guy looked like Mr. Fast Track himself. Martini glass in one hand, crisp white shirt, paisley tie, hair so perfectly styled it hardly looked real. The only thing out of sync was his expression. The fellow was mad.

And so was Samantha. Spitting mad.

The two stood eye to eye, glaring at each other. His lips moved, then hers. Wade couldn't hear them, but he bet they were hurling their share of four-letter words back and forth. Then Mr. F. T. set down his glass and stretched his hands toward Samantha in a supplicating gesture. The change in tactics didn't work. She shook her head and turned away. Her guest put his hands on her shoulders and spun her back.

Wade started toward the front door, protective instincts humming. He didn't give a damn what Samantha and the fellow's relationship was or what their argument was about. No way would he give this guy a chance to manhandle her.

He'd gone no more than two steps, when Samantha reacted. She fixed her guest with a look that would have frozen the devil himself, and the man's hands dropped to his sides. So much for her needing protection.

Wade stepped back into the shadows and watched Samantha's visitor grab his jacket, sling it over his shoulder and stalk off. A moment later, Wade heard the door slam and saw the guy stomp toward the driveway. Soon the roar of an engine indicated that he'd taken off. Inside the house, Samantha was no longer in sight.

Wade waited a good ten minutes before he strolled up to the door and rang the bell. Samantha opened the door, looking as cool and composed as if she'd spent the last half hour doing needlepoint instead of engaging in a shouting match. She was wearing a pale blue flowered silk blouse and matching split skirt that came nearly to her ankles, long crystal earrings and a musky perfume that immediately sent Wade's hormones into overdrive.

"Wade, come in," she said, and he followed her through the entry hall into a living room with thick carpeting and elegant furnishings. The silk skirt swished about her legs as she walked. "Would you like a martini?" she asked.

He noted that the pitcher on the bar was full and that her former visitor's glass had been removed from the coffee table. "I'll have ginger ale if you have some," he said.

Wade sprawled on the couch while Samantha went to the kitchen. She returned with his ginger ale and poured herself a martini. When she handed him his glass, he noticed a long, thin scar running across the back of her left hand. He wondered briefly where she'd gotten it, then her scent—not potent or overpowering, but subtly provocative—washed over him and he forgot everything else. Nick would be tempted to set his glass down, pull her into his arms and explore all her pulse points. Wade was mightily tempted, too, but he was more gentlemanly than Nick.

Samantha took a manila folder from the end table. "I have the information you wanted." She sat beside him, giving him a close-up view of the sheen of her hair, the length of her eyelashes.

Attraction and anger clashed inside him. Anger was the victor, for the moment. He would give half his book advance to kiss her, but working with her would be intolerable. He'd better stop ogling her and start pretending to indulge her desire to play detective. When the going got rough, she'd back off.

He opened the folder. "Number one. Jake Merchant. Tru-Tex Foods."

"He and Granddad have been competitors for fifty years," Samantha said.

"Tru-Tex doesn't make chili, though, do they?"

"No, Jake's never been able to come up with one that consumers like. He was in the food business five years before Granddad started Down Home. He tried to buy the original chili recipe, but my grandfather refused to sell. Then he introduced a chili of his own and it failed miserably. It still galls Jake that Granddad started later and surpassed him."

"Okay, number two," Wade said and glanced at the list and laughed. "Arnold Stewart, the restaurant critic for the Houston *Express?* He wouldn't be caught dead eating chili."

"Oh, yes, he would," Samantha said. "His haute cuisine air is for the newspaper. At heart, he's a home-cooking enthusiast. And he's opening a restaurant."

Wade shook his head. "I can't believe it."

"It's true." She leaned closer to turn over the sheet of paper and Wade lost his train of thought. She had a beauty mark just below her ear, the only flaw in the otherwise perfect column of her neck. Not really a flaw, but an imperfection that made her all the more enticing, all the more tantalizing. Contemplating Samantha's neck distracted him and he almost missed the next name on the list.

"Garrett Franklin is the president of Franklin Foods. He's been courting K and M, the same company Granddad's negotiating with, but our company's made a better offer. I'm sure Garrett would give anything to get Granddad out of the picture. He's known for fighting dirty."

"Mmm, I'm not surprised. I've heard of him." Franklin was in his forties, twice divorced, a dedicated ladies' man and a corporate shark.

"That's it for competitors."

"And inside the company?"

She quickly went over the three men with access to the recipe file, all of them company vice presidents, then added, "Granddad only listed one other person—Helen Kay. She heads the research and development department."

Wade doubted that a company the size of Down Home Foods had only four employees who couldn't be trusted. He'd undoubtedly turn up others. Meanwhile . . . "Tell me about Helen Kay."

Samantha kicked off one shoe, let the other dangle from her foot. "Helen's a home economist. She helped develop our new Hotter Than Hot Chili. She's one of the few people who knows all the ingredients."

"Which makes her vulnerable to competitors' propositions," Wade concluded.

Samantha nodded. "Any further questions?"

"Not about the list."

"What then?"

"About you."

She stiffened. "I don't see how information about me can help you."

Prickly about her privacy, was she? He gave her an easy smile. "I like to know who I'm working with." She still looked uncomfortable, but she didn't object, so he asked, "What kind of photography do you do?"

"I did studio work exclusively until I began helping out the P.I. in Dallas. But," she added quickly, "I can take action shots as well as anyone. I can use the camera for surveillance, too."

You'll never get to that point if I can help it, Wade thought. He reached over and brushed a finger over the back of her hand. "How'd you get the scar?"

Her voice chilled. "That's personal."

"Sorry. I won't ask any more questions . . . for now." He could think of plenty more he wanted to know, but he'd wait.

She picked up his glass and went to the bar, where she replenished his drink from a half-empty bottle of ginger ale. Wade followed. "What's next?" she asked, handing him the refilled glass.

"Every one of the people on that list has a reason to want your grandfather's recipe. Next step is to establish who wants it most and who could have accessed the computer file to take it. Helen the home economist is a good bet."

"I'm working in her department this summer. And I know Garrett Franklin socially. I could encourage him—"

"No!" He hadn't intended to be so vehement, but the thought of her anywhere near that lecher made him sick to his stomach.

Samantha blinked. "Why not?"

"I told you, I know plenty about Franklin. Give him a choice between a beautiful woman and a million dollars, and the money would win hands down. The guy's after K and M Frozen Foods. This isn't the right time for a relationship with Clint Brewster's granddaughter."

"I wouldn't bet on that." She tossed her head. "He'd be attracted—"

"Not now."

"—by the risk."

Though he felt a sudden affinity for the guy who'd lost his temper with Samantha earlier, Wade controlled himself as he carefully set his glass on the bar. "Listen, baby, we're not snapping pictures here—we're playing hardball. What do you think Franklin would do if he figured out what you were up to?"

"I guess we'd have to wait and see."

Damn, she was stubborn. "By that time, it would be too late." She'd be in danger. At the thought, his insides clutched with fear. The memory of Peter, his late partner, taking a bullet in the chest was still too raw, the guilt still too intense. Everything had gone wrong that day. He'd taken one drink too many, his reflexes had been too slow, he hadn't planned carefully. He'd failed Peter, but he wouldn't let it happen again. Especially not with Samantha. He put his hand on her arm. "How would you protect yourself?"

She laid her other hand on his. *Nice*, he thought. She squeezed his hand gently. *Very nice*.

"Like this," she whispered.

The next thing he knew, he was lying flat on his back on the floor.

When the little black spots dancing before his eyes cleared, he saw her standing over him. She looked like a warrior woman, golden and strong, her fists clenched, her eyes alight with triumph. He blinked at her, blinked again. *God, you're gorgeous*. Still trying to catch his breath, he gazed up at her. "You remind me of an Amazon. Where'd you learn that move?"

"Self-defense course. I'd be foolish to go into private investigating without knowing how to take care of myself."

"I underestimated you, Sam."

"Yes, you did." She stretched out her hand. "Want some help getting up?"

He considered accepting her offer and showing her a move of his own, then changed his mind. "No, thanks. I'll manage." He pulled himself to his feet. The room swayed a bit so he held on to the edge of the bar. "Well," he said, "it's been an enlightening evening."

"You're not thinking of leaving," she said.

"Are you asking me to stay?"

"Darn right I am. We haven't finished talking about the next step."

He'd hoped she'd forgotten about that. No such luck. Wade returned to the couch. "Franklin's the most likely outside candidate. I'll start with him, and I'll keep looking for the guys who entered the chili cook-off."

"What about me?"

"Nose around and see what you can find out about Helen the home economist—personal life, problems, anything that might lead her to sell out to a competitor."

"Okay." Sam gazed thoughtfully into the distance. "She leaves right at five-thirty every day. Tomorrow I'll stay late and take a look at her files."

"Good," Wade said. "I'll be at your office at five forty-five. We'll look at them together."

He could see her bristling already. "Why?"

"Safety."

"My safety?" Sam's eyes narrowed with that warrior-woman look again. "Want another demo, Phillips?"

"No, thanks." He glanced at the spot on the floor where he'd so recently lain. "I also want to check the log on the recipe file, see who's called it up lately." That seemed to pacify Sam. "By the way," he added, "what kind of work are you doing for Helen?"

"Photographing dishes for a Down Home cookbook." She rose and glanced toward the door. "I'll see you tomorrow."

Now that they'd finished their business, Wade suddenly wanted to stay a while, maybe have another drink and some quiet conversation. He opened his mouth to suggest it, but realized his head hurt. He put an exploratory hand to the back of his skull and found an egg-size lump. Better forget the conversation, go home and take a couple of aspirin. He eased up from the couch. At the front door, he turned and grinned at Sam. "Thanks for an interesting experience."

She grinned back. "Anytime."

As he walked back to his car, he thought that the next time he was flat on the floor, he'd like Sam there with him, soft and willing in his arms.

SAM EYED HELEN KAY across the plate of jalapeño corn muffins. The home economist was a well-groomed, moderately attractive woman in her mid-forties with pale skin, large brown eyes and reddish brown hair styled in a soft pageboy. She favored understated jewelry and tailored suits in neutral colors. Sam thought Helen should try to wear something brighter, jazz herself up a little. She could be quite pretty, given the right clothing and accessories. But Sam's job was not to reason why Helen preferred to blend with the woodwork . . . or come to think of it, maybe it was.

"What do you think of the table setting?" Sam asked. She'd selected a Mexican-style glazed-pottery plate for the muffins and positioned it on a bright blue cloth. A neatly folded orange napkin lay beside the plate.

Helen considered the table. "It needs a little something."

Sam nodded, left the room and returned with an arrangement of orange, yellow and blue crepe-paper flowers for the center of the table.

"Perfect," Helen said, giving Sam a warm smile. "I saw the pictures you took of the barbecued ribs. You're very talented."

"Thanks." Sam had already set up her camera equipment, and, as Helen watched, she framed the first shot. "You know, there are advantages to photographing food over people," she remarked.

"It stays in one place," Helen said.

"Yes, and it doesn't start a conversation in the middle of a shot or have embarrassing accidents like babies do." She pressed the shutter and began setting up for the next shot. "If only you could eat it when you're done." She eyed the goodies, which had been sprayed to make them look perfect.

"As a matter of fact, you can. We have a second batch," Helen said.

"No kidding. Which good fairy made the extras?"

"I did. I came in early to do the baking."

Sam moved the plate to the left and smoothed the cloth. "Do you cook in your spare time, too?"

Helen shrugged. "Occasionally."

"Down-home–type dinners?"

"French."

"Well, at least that's a change," Sam said. "How *do* you spend your spare time?"

"Oh, this and that." Helen fell silent. Sam launched into an enthusiastic summary of her own interests in hopes of drawing Helen out, but the department head's responses continued to be depressingly laconic. As Sam had been told by others in the department, Helen was warm and supportive with her staff but unremittingly closemouthed about her personal life.

Sam bit her lip in frustration. She'd managed to pick up some gossip about Helen from one of the company nutritionists and had learned that Helen had once been married to a prominent ear, nose and throat specialist. Dr. Steven Kay had reportedly left Helen for a well-heeled patient with clogged sinuses and a great-looking pair of tonsils. Sam wondered if Helen was in the market for a replacement for the good doctor or if she'd decided one husband was enough. Did she spend her evenings out on the town or at home inventing new recipes for Down Home Foods? Or perhaps concocting ways to poison her scoundrel of an ex-husband by sending him a bowl of arsenic-laced chili? Helen certainly wasn't going to supply the answer.

By the time she'd finished photographing the food and Helen had returned to her office, Sam was ready to spit nails. All she'd gained from an investment of thirty minutes snacking on the extra muffins were several hundred calories and the news that Helen Kay preferred white wine over red—certainly not an incriminating fact.

Tonight *had* to be better.

She broke another muffin in half and buttered it, then headed back to her office. Maybe she and Wade would discover something interesting in Helen's files. It irked her that Wade insisted on being present when she checked them. She didn't need his help. Copying a few disks was a simple task. When the hotshot detective appeared, she'd show him a thing or two.

She had to admit, though, that her cousin Tonya was right. There was something about him—a wicked twinkle in his sapphire-blue eyes, a lazy smile and a tone of voice that told a woman he knew what she wanted and how to give it to her.

Hmmph! What *she* wanted, Sam reminded herself, was her own detective agency. She'd had quite enough of entanglements with unsuitable males for the moment, thank you.

There'd been Frank, who'd been less interested in Sam than in the Brewster millions; Martin, who'd seemed perfect until Sam discovered one small flaw—he had a wife and three kids;

and several others who'd simply bored her silly after a while. No, she'd sworn off romantic involvements for now, maybe forever.

She opened the door of the utilitarian room that served as her office. Her desk sat in the center, surrounded on two sides by walls of shelves crowded with books and pamphlets on photography and food. She'd covered the third wall with cork, upon which she'd tacked photos for the upcoming cookbook. Across from her desk was a straight chair and behind it the door. Not a very inspiring space for a photographer, but Sam guessed it was okay for a detective.

As if her thoughts of involvement with the wrong men had conjured him up, Keith Nelson, Sam's most recent mistake, appeared at her office door. "Samantha," he said in a well-modulated voice that always made her think he should have been a disc jockey instead of the assistant marketing director for a food company, "let me take you to dinner."

"No, Keith."

"You can take me, then." He smiled, displaying tooth-paste-commercial teeth.

"No again," Sam said, annoyance creeping into her voice. "I thought I made my feelings clear, especially after what you said last night." He'd insisted that her breaking up with him was the reason he'd been passed over for a promotion. Ridiculous!

Keith ignored the reference to the night before, took the chair across from her desk and settled in, filling the room with the scent of expensive cologne. "I know a new place—very trendy. Nuevo Southwestern. You love that kind of food."

Sam was a sucker for goat cheese, black beans and blue corn, but not that much of a sucker. "Why put either one of us through this?" she said, trying to be patient. "I told you, our relationship's over."

He smiled. "You know what they say—'It's not over till the f—'"

"Keith," she said gently, "the fat lady sang months ago. We're through."

He reached across the desk and took her hand, imprisoning it between both of his. "Because we had a long-distance romance," he said earnestly. "Now that you're in Houston, we can make it work." Sam tried to slide her hand away, but he held her fast. "The Chamber of Commerce is having a dinner dance at the Houston Yacht Club Saturday."

"I know, but—"

"Come with me."

"No. Listen to me, Keith. We have absolutely nothing to gain by going to the dance or anywhere else together. Besides, I'm going—"

"Besides, she's going with me," a lazy drawl interrupted.

Startled, Sam looked up to see Wade Phillips filling the doorway.

He advanced into the cramped room. "Right, doll?"

Sam shot him a killing look for the *doll.* "Right."

Since Keith had appropriated the room's only chair, Wade sat on the corner of Sam's desk. "Wade Phillips," he said to Keith and stretched out a hand.

Keith had no choice but to drop Sam's hand and take Wade's. "Keith Nelson," he muttered.

The contrast between the two men was striking, Sam thought. Soft versus hard. Smooth versus rough. Keith, an ad from *Gentlemen's Quarterly* in his gray Pierre Cardin suit, his crisp white shirt and power tie; Wade, a modern version of the lone cowboy, lean and tough in worn jeans and chambray shirt rolled up to the elbows. She'd like to take a shot of Wade leaning against a fence, a craggy mountain in the background. She'd like to take a shot *at* him. Doll indeed!

Wade smiled at Keith. "Sam and I are headin' out for some chicken-fried steak. Care to join us?"

Keith grimaced and stood. "No, thanks."

"Another time," Wade said, his drawl growing more pronounced as he slid off the desk and turned to Sam. "Ready, darlin'?"

Sam nodded. She wriggled into her shoes and walked around the other side of the desk. With a proprietary air, Wade straightened the collar of Sam's silk blouse, then put his arm around her waist. She wanted to deck him again, but Keith still stood in the room watching. Instead, she patted Wade's cheek . . . a bit harder than necessary. "I'll go freshen my makeup. Be right back, *darlin'*."

In the rest room, as she fluffed her hair and applied fresh lipstick, Sam's temper cooled. After all, Wade had gotten her out of a sticky situation. She'd have to thank him for that. When she rejoined him in the hallway, she did. "I appreciate your rescuing me."

"No problem. I'm a knight in shining armor. What time shall I pick you up Saturday?"

Sam took a step back. "You . . . you don't really have to—"

"Sure I do. A Chamber of Commerce bash is just the place where everyone on that list your granddad gave us would likely turn up."

She couldn't argue with that. "Seven o'clock. It's, uh, black-tie."

Wade's lips curved at her tone. "Don't worry, darlin', I won't embarrass you. I'll stop off and buy a black tie to go with my jeans." His grin broadened as Sam's cheeks flushed. Then becoming serious, he said, "We have work to do."

Sam lowered her voice. "Helen left the office half an hour ago. We can get started on her files."

He leaned an elbow against the wall. "Can we?"

She frowned at his tone. "Why not?"

"Aren't you forgetting something?"

"The key to her office. I have a master." Sam fished in her pocket and held it up.

"The cleaning crew. Lesson one in being a private eye, darlin'. Always make sure the cleaning crew's out of the way before you ransack an office."

How could she have forgotten that? Unwilling to admit she hadn't thought of the cleaning service, she improvised. "I thought I heard them a while ago."

"Uh-uh," Wade said. He gestured toward a nearby office. "Trash cans haven't been emptied."

"Oh." Sam blushed again. Great way to impress the ace detective with her powers of observation.

"I'll check the computer system while we wait," Wade said, "and see if anyone's accessed the recipe file lately."

Meekly, she led Wade back to her office and sat across the desk from him.

He flipped on her computer. "I'll use the login and password of someone with supervisory rights." He pulled a sheet of paper from his pocket, consulted it and began punching keys, seeming to forget Sam's presence as he concentrated on his task.

Sam concentrated on him. Perhaps because he was a tall, broad-shouldered man, he dominated the small room in a way that Keith never could. Wade looked like the kind of guy who'd be more comfortable in a deer blind or a corral than a high-tech environment, yet he seemed thoroughly at home with the computer. Even his fingers on the keyboard looked lean and strong, in contrast to Keith's pale, fleshy ones. Wade's hands were bare; Keith still wore his college ring, decorated with his fraternity crest, for goodness' sake. Sam watched Wade's fingers race effortlessly over the keys. She suspected he would be at ease anywhere and wondered how he'd look in black-tie.

The janitorial staff arrived and left; Wade hardly glanced up, only muttered under his breath then turned on Sam's printer. Sam watched paper spew out. A few minutes later, she said, "I could start in Helen's office while you finish here."

He shook his head. "Cleaning crew's still on this floor. I haven't—"

"—heard the elevator," Sam finished, and he looked up, grinning at her.

Ten minutes later, they heard the elevator signal ding and the doors open and close. "Okay," Wade said.

"What did you find out?" Sam asked as they headed for Helen's office.

"Something interesting. See right here." He held up a newly printed sheet. "Someone with the login 12LONGFIVE called up that file at 11:00 p.m., July 21." Wade pointed to the list Clint's secretary had provided. "Let's see. That's Ray Donovan, vice president of sales and marketing."

"Uncle Ray?" Sam said.

"He's a relative?"

"No, he's Granddad's oldest friend. He's been here since Down Home started. He'd never steal anything—"

"Don't be so sure."

"I am sure. Ray owns enough shares in the company that he'd lose more than he'd gain by taking the recipe. Besides, he never works late. He's home in bed by eleven o'clock."

Wade seemed unimpressed. "I want to add a tracking system to computer security so if it ever happens again, we'll know which machine was used to access the recipe file. Meanwhile, see if you can find out what Ray was up to around July 21."

"All right." At least he'd entrusted her with some small responsibility. She smiled as she unlocked Helen's office.

They entered the room. This corner office was a marked contrast to Sam's. Large and airy, it was furnished with an attractive off-white couch and two comfortable navy side chairs. Two wide windows on one wall looked out on a forested area that Sam's grandfather had insisted on keeping in its pristine state. A window on the other wall faced the parking lot. Helen's large oak desk sat at the opposite side of the room, facing the couch. Quickly, Sam stepped in front of Wade and took the desk chair. "I'll look. After all, this was my idea."

"Be my guest." He slouched on the sofa across the room and watched her.

Feeling Wade's eyes boring into her, Sam rummaged through Helen's paraphernalia. Tonight was important, the first real opportunity she'd had to function as a private investigator. She knew she had the ability, but she needed to convince Wade. She'd shown him she had the muscle, she thought, grinning to herself; now she had to demonstrate her investigative skills.

She'd been so anxious to meet him, the cream of the private-investigating crop, and to impress him with her enthusiasm and skill. He'd been impressed, all right, but not the way she wanted. Those blue eyes of his had raked over her with masculine appreciation when they'd met, but she didn't need to add Wade Phillips's name to her list of admirers. She wanted to work with him, not play. In spite of his bedroom eyes and sexy body. The heck with his charms. She wanted to be his colleague, his peer. And she would. Even if she had to flatten him again to accomplish it. She kicked off her shoes and went to work.

The first desk drawer yielded nothing; neither did any of the others. All she discovered was what she already knew to be true—Helen was neat and organized. She opened a cabinet next, reached into the back and extracted a file of computer diskettes. "Voilà!" she cried, holding up the box.

Wade walked across the room and leaned over her shoulder. He smelled of soap and leather. And man. Sam felt a shiver make its way up her spine as he put one warm hand on her shoulder and leaned closer. "Recipes, Staff, Schedules," he read as she flipped through the disks. His voice fitted him, Sam thought. Deep and rough, it belonged to the night. If he could give a woman shivers when he read off a list of labels, imagine what might happen when . . .

Focus, Sam, she ordered herself, and checked the next disk.

"Pay dirt," Wade said. The label read Personal, as did the following four. "Let's copy them and get out of here. Did you bring extra disks?"

Sam flipped on the computer and inserted Helen's first disk. "Didn't need to. I've set up a file on the main computer. It's highly restricted. Helen will never be able to access it." She knew she was gloating, but she couldn't help it.

"I guess being Clint Brewster's granddaughter has its advantages," Wade said.

His hand still lay on her shoulder. Sam told herself to ignore it. She worked quickly, getting into the rhythm—insert disk, copy, pull out disk.

"Hold it!" Wade's grasp tightened as she shoved in disk number four.

"Wha—" Sam turned to gape at him, but he silenced her with a finger to his lips. She heard a sound from down the hall and held her breath. The elevator doors! The cleaning crew must have forgotten something.

Wade leaned around her, yanked out the disk and turned off the computer. Sam jumped up, and as she did, glanced out the window. Below them, in the parking lot, sat a car she recognized. Helen's!

"Oh my God!" Heels were clicking down the hall. "Helen's back," she whispered. "We have to get out of here."

Wade shoved the disk file into the cabinet. "No time."

Sam's eyes darted around the room. "Where . . . ?"

"Behind the couch." He pushed her ahead of him and they dived for the floor. Wade landed half on top of Sam, then rolled behind her an instant before the door opened and Helen entered the room. Sam struggled to hold her breath.

Helen glanced at the lights and frowned. "Cleaning crew," she mumbled, then strode to the desk. Sam watched, trying not to tremble, as Helen set her briefcase on the desk and unlocked it. What if she turned and saw them?

Don't move, Sam ordered herself. *Don't even breathe.* Behind her, she felt the reassuring heat of Wade's body, the steady thump of his heart. He held her fast, with one arm thrown across her, just below her breasts. Sam concentrated on remaining still, but it wasn't easy. In front of her, Helen rummaged in her desk. In back of her lay Wade. They were practically glued together, so close she felt his every breath. She felt his body harden, throb against her. There was no mistaking his arousal. Her heart began to pound.

Suddenly, Wade's arm tightened around her. He leaned closer and his breath rasped in her ear. "Your shoes," he whispered.

Shoes? What was he talking about? Baffled, Sam wiggled her toes...her *bare* toes. *Oh, no!* Sam's eyes shot back to the desk. Beneath it, inches from where Helen was standing, lay a pair of white sandals, the shoes Sam had kicked off minutes ago.

3

A TRICKLE OF COLD SWEAT ran down Sam's chest. She let out a hiccuping breath.

Wade's arm gripped her like a steel band. "Keep quiet," he whispered in her ear. "And pray."

She prayed. Fervently, intently, while her muscles screamed with tension and her eyes locked on Helen in horrified fascination.

The scene before her played out in excruciatingly slow motion. Helen opened the cabinet. Reached inside. Pulled out the disk file and removed a handful of disks. Put them in a carrier, dropped the carrier into her briefcase and snapped it shut. She picked up the case. Without so much as a glance at the floor, she turned and left, flipping off the light and shutting the door behind her.

Sam felt as if she were made of jelly, as if every muscle had collapsed. Wade sat up, but Sam remained in a heap on the floor.

"Lesson two," said the voice behind her, "never leave a calling card when breaking and entering."

"I'll come in barefoot next time," she managed to say.

Wade stood. "Come on, Nancy Drew. You don't have time to swoon. Go check out the files and see what she took."

At his derisive tone, Sam's energy returned, along with a surge of anger. She sprang up and faced him, hands fisted. "Okay, but don't tell me you weren't scared, too. Your heart was going like a trip-hammer. I could feel it." *Along with other things.* But she wouldn't think of that now.

His mouth grim, Wade said, "Sure I was scared, but I make damn certain I don't have to be very often."

Sam looked down. "Sorry about the shoes."

He tipped up her chin and held her gaze. "Apology accepted," he said softly. He paused a moment, then added, "The, uh, first time I went through someone's apartment was a long time ago, back in my smoking days. The fellow showed up and when I ran for the closet, I left a burning cigarette in the ashtray."

Sam laughed, not sure whether he'd told her the truth or concocted a story to make her feel better. "What happened?"

"Nothing. He'd drunk too much to notice. He tossed his jacket on the floor, sat down on the couch, picked up the cigarette and took a puff. Guess he thought it was his."

Her equilibrium restored, Sam went to Helen's desk and found the disk file. "She took the personal disks, of course. At least we made a start. We can go back to my office and read what we have."

"Leave it for tomorrow. We've had enough excitement tonight." He glanced at his watch. "And I have to be somewhere in half an hour. Put on your shoes and let's get out of here."

Sam didn't argue. Wade walked her to her car and opened the door. "Drive carefully." In a surprisingly gentle gesture, he caught an errant strand of her hair and tucked it behind her ear. "Call me tomorrow after you read the files."

As she watched him stride off into the darkness, Sam wondered where he had to be. And with whom.

ABSENTLY RAKING his fingers through his already tousled hair, Wade paced his study. He'd left Sam and headed for the office of Alan McKenzie, the executive he'd been following these past few weeks. McKenzie, whom Wade had dubbed

Don Juanito due to his five foot seven inches, worked late on Thursdays then played, selecting his partner from a seemingly endless array of choices. The latest playmate of the week had been a statuesque redhead, three inches taller than Juanito and a good twenty years younger. They'd parted around two-thirty and Wade had driven home, planning to fall into bed.

But sleep had eluded him and he'd come in here to write. So far, he hadn't gotten more than a few words on the screen. Sam kept intruding. God, the woman gave him a pain in his nether region. Taking off her shoes! Leaving them in plain sight! She'd never succeed as a private investigator. Another stupid mistake like the one she'd made tonight and she'd get herself busted for breaking and entering.

She was beautiful, he thought, feeling another type of pain, the ache of arousal. Just thinking about her made him as hard as Nick Petrelli's .38. When he'd lain beside her a while ago, the soft undersides of her breasts grazing his arm, the silk of her hair brushing his cheeks, all he could think of was having her, right there behind the couch with Helen Kay standing ten feet away. He closed his eyes and remembered how well Sam fit in his arms. He remembered the scent of her skin. She hadn't worn perfume this evening, but still she'd smelled like summer flowers.

Wade cursed. This was no way to solve a case. This was no way to finish his book . . . or maybe it was. Turning back to the computer, he took out his frustrations on the keyboard as Allison a.k.a. Al McGuire and Nick lay in a tangled heap on the floor behind the couch in Randall Porter's office:

"He's gone," Al breathed. "And he didn't see us," she added as if she couldn't believe it. "We're okay."

"Yeah, we're okay," Nick murmured. "We're perfect." To his way of thinking, they couldn't be in a better position. And he was in no hurry to change their situation.

He raised himself onto one elbow and leaned over her. "You know," he drawled, "when I first saw you, darlin', I thought *you* were perfect, but you're not." Her eyebrows shot up, and he continued, "You've got a chipped tooth... right there." He parted her lips with his finger and slipped it inside to touch the tiny flaw. "And you've got a beauty mark at the corner of your mouth." He flicked his tongue over it, heard her gasp and forgot the game. Hell, this close to Al, he forgot the case he was on, the universe he was in. With a groan of desire, he pulled her closer and took what he wanted.

"WADE, I've found something! Wade, are you there?" Sam shouted into the phone.

"Yeah, here."

His voice was raspy with sleep, and Sam wondered how late he'd been out last night. "Did you hear me?"

"Yeah. Y'found something."

Clearly, he wasn't a morning person. But maybe he listened better than he talked. She'd start with the easy stuff, give him time to wake up. "I checked on Ray Donovan."

Wade responded with a grunt that sounded like, "Go on."

"He was away on a cruise the week of July twenty-first."

"That doesn't excuse him. Maybe he tapped in via modem." Wade yawned. "If you find out anything else, call me later... afternoon."

"No! I found something important on Helen's personal disk." She'd almost given up when she discovered it. After three hours of reading Helen's files, she'd decided that the home economist's life was about as exciting as an egg custard. She'd learned that Helen wore size 8B shoes and size-twelve dresses, that she shopped at Macy's, had two capped front teeth and had recently had a disagreement with the mechanic who worked on her car.

Sam had almost decided to skip the last file, but that wouldn't be good investigative work. She called it up and got the shock of her life.

"This is titled Notes," she told Wade. "What she's written here seems to be a diary of some sort. Listen. 'I am lonely and desperate. Loretta's illness cost me everything I had. I need cash. Who can I turn to?'

"That's dated three weeks before Granddad discovered that the recipe had been stolen. And here's the next one, two days later. 'I have nothing to sustain me but my pride. If I do this thing, soon even that will be gone. What I'm planning is wrong. Will I be able to live with the guilt? I toss and turn at night, I pray for an alternative, but nothing materializes. I have no options. I will do it.'"

"Jeez!" Wade said, his voice clear now. "Any more?"

"Just one—'We met last night and made the deal. I can't turn back now.'"

"Incriminating as hell. I'll have to tail her," Wade said. "Damn, I can't tonight."

"I will," Sam said.

"The hell you will."

"The hell I won't," she countered. "I'm perfectly capable of following Helen. I know how to be unobtrusive."

Wade muttered something she couldn't hear. "You better. You have a car phone?"

"Yes."

"Give me the number." She did, and he continued, "Call me immediately if you have any trouble."

"I won't have any," Sam said.

"Call me when you get home."

"Okay."

"I don't like the idea of your going out alone," Wade said, "but I can't do anything about it. Just keep your eyes open."

Sam sighed with exaggerated patience. "I will."

"Oh, and, darlin', don't forget to keep your shoes on."

AT FIVE-THIRTY that evening, Sam left the office and pulled onto the freeway a few lengths behind Helen Kay's car. Sam felt a rush of adrenaline, the same high she'd experienced her junior year in prep school when, on a dare, she'd sneaked into the dean of women's quarters, snitched the formidable woman's wig and placed it on the statue of the school's founder.

Remembering the incident, Sam laughed aloud. Tonight would be as much fun. Private investigating beat photographing simpering debutantes by a mile. She turned on her radio and as she cruised down the freeway, sang along with Natalie Cole.

Once she'd parked in an inconspicuous spot across from Helen's neat brick house, excitement waned quickly. Sam checked her camera, then took a pair of high-powered binoculars from the glove compartment and trained them on the house.

Nothing happened. Occasionally, Helen passed through the living room, but other than that, Sam saw no activity. No one went in; Helen didn't come out. Eventually, the home economist went into the living room and sat in an armchair, sipping iced tea and reading from a sheaf of papers in her lap. Boring!

Sam was disappointed. She'd hoped to impress Wade with a stunning discovery, get this case solved with lightning speed. She waited until Helen stood up, yawned and put the papers on the coffee table. Obviously, she was going to bed.

Sam drove off, intending to go home and sack out herself, when the thought occurred to her that Helen might have left her disks at the office again. Wouldn't hurt to swing by and take a look.

The corporate-headquarters building, so inviting during the day with its glass facade that reflected the forested surroundings, now looked forbidding. Sam hesitated a moment before getting out of her car, checked her purse for the can of Mace she carried, then squared her shoulders and walked across the deserted parking lot.

The security guard met her at the door. "Ms. Brewster, what're you doin' here so late at night?"

"I left something in my office," she said easily as he let her in. She took the elevator to her floor, scurried down the hall and slipped into Helen's office. She didn't want to take a chance on the guard's seeing a light go on in an office that wasn't hers, so she shone a penlight into the cabinet where she'd found Helen's disks last night. She found the container, but no personal disks were in it.

"Damn!" She'd wasted an hour coming over here, but reminded herself that this was part of an investigator's life. You had to try everything, leave no stone unturned. Unfortunately, nothing was under this stone.

Sam plodded back to her car. Home was an hour away. She hoped she could stay awake.

WADE GLANCED at his watch as he opened his front door. Twelve-fifteen. The meeting with his client, Carole McKenzie, wife of the executive he was following, had lasted longer than he'd expected. She'd gotten a phone call last night—mild threats interspersed with heavy breathing, and she'd been upset. Did Wade think her husband might be responsible? What could the call mean? He didn't know. It could mean a lot of things, or it could mean nothing. They'd spent a long time considering the possibilities.

He went into his study, thinking that Sam was undoubtedly home and fast asleep by now. She'd probably called and left a message.

He checked his answering machine. No messages. Maybe she'd forgotten to call. He dialed her home number. On the fourth ring, her machine picked up. Then he dialed her carphone number. It gave him a recording. "The customer you are trying to reach is unavailable or out of the service area."

Wade hung up and turned on his computer. His creative juices always flowed best at night.

Half an hour later, he finished a scene, rubbed the back of his neck, stretched and looked at his watch. Damn. Sam still hadn't called and it was nearly one o'clock. He called her home and car phone again. No answer.

She had to be somewhere. He could go out and look, but in a city the size of Houston, he might as well be looking for a grain of sand in the desert.

He began to pace. Had something happened to her? The specter of Peter rose before him—overconfident, too inexperienced to know when to pull out of a situation that had grown perilous. Peter had paid with his life. Would Samantha—

No, that didn't bear thinking about. He grabbed the phone once more, shook it when she didn't answer.

Five minutes. He'd give her five minutes, and then—

His telephone rang. "Yeah."

"Wade, this is Sam. I just got in."

"Damn it, where've you been?" he growled. "I've been calling your house and your car every fifteen minutes."

"Why?"

"I was worried about you." He took a breath, steadied himself. "Why didn't you pick up in the car?"

"I didn't hear a ring. The, uh, battery in my car phone must be dead." She sounded sheepish.

"Get a new one." Now that he knew she was safe, he asked, "Did you find out anything?"

She gave him a brief rundown of her evening. "And I went back to the office and checked, but the personal disks were gone."

"You were at your office?" he shouted, incredulous. "In a dark, deserted building? Were you alone?"

"Of course not. We have a security guard on the premises all night."

"Unless he stood beside you while you rifled through Helen's files, you were alone."

"Don't be such a grouch," she snapped. "How many times have *you* been in a building alone?"

"That's different."

"Chauvinist," Sam muttered.

"We'll discuss that later," Wade said. "Did you find anything else?"

"Nothing." She sighed.

He couldn't do anything after the fact. On the other hand, maybe he'd throttle her later. He yawned loudly. "It's after one. Get some sleep and I'll see you tonight."

"Tonight?"

"Chamber of Commerce, remember? Black-tie. Seven o'clock."

"Oh, sure."

He could tell by her voice she'd forgotten. Good thing he'd reminded her. He told her good-night, hung up and rubbed his temple. Head beginning to throb, he shuffled into his bedroom. God, Samantha Brewster was something! Going into a building alone. Not checking her car-phone battery. If she kept up like this, she'd give him tension headaches, an ulcer and high blood pressure combined. The woman was a disaster about to happen.

SAM SLEPT LATE, did her yoga routine, then spent the day running errands. She returned home just in time to get ready for the evening. She chose a lace dress with thin shoulder straps in café au lait, slipped into bone-colored sandals and pinned up her hair. At seven on the nose, the doorbell rang and Sam went to answer.

With an effort, she kept her mouth from dropping open. Wade was gorgeous. In a midnight-black tux, with his raven hair and sapphire-blue eyes, he looked like the devil incarnate. Had he made some crack the other night about buying a black tie? The attire he was wearing this evening had obviously been tailored just for him. She swallowed. "Hello."

He looked at her, every inch of her, with a thoroughness that was both disconcerting and thrilling. "You're stunning," he murmured in a voice that sounded awestruck.

Sam smiled. "Thanks. So are you. Black's your color." When he raised an eyebrow in question, she added, "It makes you look dangerous."

He took her hand and drew her outside. "I *am* dangerous." Not relinquishing his hold on her, he led her across the lawn.

They reached the driveway, and he opened the door of a silver BMW. The man was full of surprises.

"Private investigating must be lucrative," Sam said.

He gave her an enigmatic smile. "It's given me a good life."

The guy she'd worked with in Dallas had driven a battered Jeep. Maybe Wade had made some shrewd investments, or perhaps he had another source of income. She got into the car and settled back in the leather seat.

He pulled out of the driveway, then turned to her. "Nervous about the evening?"

"No," Sam replied. "Why should I be?"

"Thought you might be uncomfortable running into the guy who was in your office the other evening."

"Not at all."

"Want to tell me about him?"

Sam considered whether to divulge this kind of personal information. Why not? Keith was over and done with and therefore no longer important. Talking about him was as harmless as discussing last week's headlines. "I was visiting my grandparents and met Keith at the company Christmas party last year. We hit it off, or seemed to, and started seeing each other when he came to Dallas or I was here. We got involved." She paused and shrugged. "Bottom line was, he wanted to get married, I didn't."

"To him or to anyone?"

"Neither, at the moment."

"Me, neither. I'm not into long-term stuff. I've had enough."

"Was your divorce messy?"

His eyes narrowed. "How'd you know I'm divorced?"

"You're not the only one who does his homework. I had you checked out." He grinned at her, and she felt a flash of triumph. "So," she prodded, "you were married?"

"Once too often." His expression was serious, almost sad.

"What went wrong?"

"Let's just say I had no way to be a P.I. and a husband at the same time. Not enough time and not enough money."

"The money part must've changed."

"Yeah, it has."

"Do you ever see your ex-wife?" Sam asked.

He gave her a puzzled glance. "You'd be more likely to see her than I would. She travels in some pretty classy circles these days, but I do run into her every now and then. Why?"

"I imagine she's sorry she didn't stick with you if income mattered so much to her."

Wade grinned. "I imagine she would be, except she snagged an extremely well-heeled oilman for husband number two." He frowned. "Is money important to you, Sam?"

"Not particularly."

"But then, you've always had plenty."

"True," she acknowledged, "but I could get along on less. Being happy with the way you spend your time is more important. Being challenged."

"Is that why you decided to go into private investigating?" He pulled onto the freeway, heading toward the bay area.

"Yes, I like photography, but I was getting bored with doing bridal portraits and taking baby pictures. I wanted something more stimulating." She didn't tell him the whole story, but it really wasn't his business.

"Detective work can be dangerous."

"I know."

"It can also be boring and frustrating. And sometimes it's plain nasty. Sleazy."

"Are you trying to scare me off, Phillips?" she asked.

"Yeah, is it working?"

"Uh-uh, I'm determined." She kicked off one shoe and dangled it by the strap. "And you're beginning to sound like my parents."

"They disapprove, do they?"

"Disapprove? They'd object to anything more dangerous than crossing the street. If they had their way, they'd lock me in a golden cage and throw away the key." Abashed that she'd spoken of her problems so openly and with such vehemence, Sam bit her lip and turned to stare out the window.

"You're the kind of person who'd find a way out of that cage," he said softly. "You already have."

Sam gave him a grateful smile. "Thanks."

"You know," he continued, "you don't look like any female P.I. I ever saw."

"Oh? What do I look like?"

He turned toward her. "A princess."

For a moment, she couldn't answer. The way he'd spoken, the look in his eyes during that brief glance, had been so potent she felt as if she'd been hit with a bolt of lightning. Thoughts scrambling, she managed to ask, "And what does a female P.I. look like?"

"Tough."

"I *am* tough, and you're being chauvinistic again."

"Sorry." Without taking his eyes from the road, he reached in his pocket, extracted a white handkerchief and waved it at her.

Sam chuckled. "Truce," she agreed.

After a moment, Wade flipped on the radio and the sounds of country-western filled the car. Now Sam relaxed. For the rest of their trip, she thought about Wade and his marriage and wondered if it had left him bitter.

Twenty minutes later, they turned into the small city of Shoreacres. Oak trees immediately gave way to palms, and a block ahead of them lay the shimmering expanse of Galveston Bay. Wade drew up before the beige stucco Houston Yacht Club. To the right, they could see the crowded marina. Behind it, white sails dotted the bay.

Inside, in the upstairs ballroom, movers and shakers from Houston's business community mingled with well-known faces from the political establishment. In the background, the current "in" orchestra, Colonel Winston and the Space Cadets, played. Sam felt at home here, but she was surprised that Wade seemed to know a fair number of the guests.

He handed her a glass of champagne from the tray of a passing waiter and declined one for himself, requesting water, instead. "There's your grandfather's rival," he said.

Sam turned and spotted Jake Merchant across the room in deep discussion with several men. Jake had aged noticeably since she'd seen him last. His hair was snow-white, his shoulders stooped. Contrasting Jake's posture with her grandfather's erect carriage, Sam found it hard to believe the two were the same age.

"He's planning to retire next year," Wade remarked, sipping his water.

Sam stared across the room at Jake and shook her head. "Clint will stay at his desk until they cart him away. I thought Jake would do the same. I wonder why he's quitting."

"Health reasons. Heart trouble. Jake's turning the company over to his two grandsons."

She gasped. "Richard and Drew?"

"Apparently."

"But," Sam said, "they're kids. Drew spends most of his time goofing off, and Richard—well, I don't think he has what it takes to run a big company. He barely made it through college. He went to some school out West—Arizona, I think—and spent most of his time on academic probation."

"They're the only grandchildren Jake has, and he wants to keep the company in the family."

"From what I know of his grandsons, they'll have trouble keeping it afloat." She frowned at Wade. "Are you sure about this? I haven't heard a word."

"P.I. rule number three, darlin'—Keep your ear to the ground." He drained his glass and set it on a nearby table. "And the corollary to the rule is, if listening doesn't work, have contacts in high places."

"Where's your contact?" she asked, interested.

"One is with the *Express*, the other's a big wheel in the Chamber of Commerce."

Sam nodded. She'd remember Wade's rule. "Speak of the devil," she remarked. "Here comes Richard Merchant now."

She drew Wade's attention to a round-faced young man ambling across the ballroom.

Richard had changed since she'd last seen him. Flab had turned to muscle, an abundance of muscle. He must spend most of his free time in a gym. She doubted his mind had shaped up along with his body, though. He probably still had a headful of putty.

"Let's waylay him," Wade suggested, and they planted themselves in his path.

"Richard," Sam said as he approached them, "how nice to see you."

Richard stopped, blinked and stared at her with pale blue eyes. "Sam?"

"Yes." She introduced Wade.

"Nice to meet you. Sorry I can't shake your hand." He held a champagne glass in one hand and a plate piled high with canapés in the other.

No wonder Richard had developed all those muscles, Sam thought. He needed to work out to burn off all the calories he consumed. "What are you doing these days?" she asked him.

He puffed out his chest. "Working for Grandfather. Learning the business. Yes, I'm getting to know every nut and bolt in the old corporation. Got to master it all, you know. Every facet."

Could he? Sam doubted it. In her opinion, Richard Merchant was all brawn, no brains.

"Rich, stop monopolizing all the lovely ladies," said a voice behind them.

Sam turned and met the eyes of Richard's brother. "Hello, Drew."

"Hello, Serena."

"Samantha. Where've you been keeping yourself, Drew?"

He gave her a rundown of his latest jaunts to exotic places. "But I'm home to stay now," he added, then excused himself and urged his brother along with him.

Sam watched them maneuver through the ballroom. The two Merchant brothers always reminded her of characters in the circus. Richard was the clown, Drew the fast-talking ringmaster whose words never amounted to much.

She turned to Wade. Keeping her voice low, she said, "Your contact was apparently right about the Merchants. Any information about the others on the list?"

Wade nodded. "Arnold Stewart. You were on target about his interest in down-home cooking and about the restaurant. In fact, it'll be opening next week. But he's changed his plans. He's a silent partner. Doesn't want to ruin his food-critic image."

They wandered through the room, stopping to talk with other guests and nibble on hors d'oeuvres. Suddenly, Sam gasped and grabbed Wade's arm. "Look!"

He followed her gaze. "Garrett Franklin. And the woman with him—"

"Is Helen," they chorused.

Sam eyed the couple, who were engaged in rapt conversation. "I never would have pictured them together." She'd thought of Helen as rather mousy, yet there she was, dressed in a low-cut turquoise gown and hanging on the arm of the city's most notorious ladies' man.

"Let's go talk to them," Wade suggested, and they strolled casually in Garrett and Helen's direction.

Sam stared at Garrett Franklin. He was a big man, tall enough to dwarf most of the men in the room, and handsome in an oily sort of way. He reeked of money, from his carefully styled hair to the diamond on his pinkie. "Sam," he cried, taking both her hands in his, "it's a pleasure to see you."

His gaze raked her from head to toe. "You're looking beautiful as always."

"Thank you, Garrett." She introduced Wade, then remarked, "Helen, I didn't know you and Garrett were friends."

"We met a couple of months ago," Helen said, smiling at Garrett.

Sam glanced at Wade. He, too, had noted the timing.

"Sam, would you like another drink?" Garrett asked, stroking her hand as he took her empty champagne glass from her. Sam sneaked a look at Helen. The woman's face was impassive. Whatever she thought about her date's flirting, her expression gave nothing away.

Sam backed up a step. "I think I'll pass."

Garrett stepped closer. "I sent you an invitation to the party I'm having to kick off the fall social season next Friday. You haven't responded."

"Sorry. It must've slipped my mind."

"This is a reminder then," he said, lowering his voice to a sexy purr and brushing a finger across her bare shoulder.

"Sam, we haven't had a chance to dance yet," Wade interrupted. He seized her arm in a possessive gesture that signaled hands off. "Nice meeting you both," he said to Garrett and Helen. "Come on, darlin'."

When they reached the dance floor and he pulled her against him, Sam chuckled. "You were a bit obvious, grabbing me like that."

"I meant to be obvious." He pulled back and stared down at her, eyes dark with anger. "That sleazeball was undressing you with his eyes. Another minute, and he'd have used his hands."

Sam laughed aloud. "You did the same thing earlier this evening, when I opened my door."

He smiled sheepishly. "That was different."

"Really? I seem to remember your telling me you were dangerous."

"I may be dangerous *at times*, but I know how to be a gentleman."

"Let's both keep that in mind," Sam said. For a moment, they were silent, swaying in time to the music, then she said, "You didn't give me a chance to respond to Garrett's invitation."

"Yeah, some invitation." He tightened his hold on her. "The guy's a rat. Keep away from him."

Sam drew back and glared at him. "Watch it, Phillips. You're giving orders again."

"Do you want to work with me, Sam, or make my life miserable?"

"Work with you, of course."

"Then take a few orders . . . please."

She couldn't help smiling at him. "At least you've said the magic word."

Wade pulled her closer and laid his cheek against hers. After a moment, he turned, and his lips grazed her temple. "Are you going to stay out of Franklin's way?"

"If you can give me a good reason."

He sighed. "Let's go outside where we can talk." He led her off the floor and out through a glass door to a wide balcony that faced the bay.

From behind them came the strains of the orchestra and the murmur of voices, but outside the night was quiet and dark. A quarter moon hung in the star-studded sky. A brisk breeze from the bay set palm leaves fluttering, reminding Sam that summer had ended. She hugged her bare shoulders.

"Cold?" Wade asked.

"A little."

He took off his jacket and slipped it around her. "Better?"

"Uh-huh." Sam stared up at the sky for a dreamy moment, then remembered why they'd come outside. Not for stargazing. "You were going to give me some reasons," she reminded him.

"We both know Garrett Franklin's hot to get the company your grandfather's negotiating with. He wants it so bad he can taste it, and I think he's ruthless enough to do just about anything to get it. I don't want you involved."

"I can take care of myself."

"Samantha," he said, "you don't have the experience to deal with a guy like Franklin—"

"I have plenty of experience," she protested.

"I meant in private investigating."

"Oh." Her face flamed, but she raised her chin. "I'm still going to the party."

Wade groaned, then said, "How about a compromise? We'll go together."

"So you can keep an eye on me?" When he nodded, she glared at him, then forced herself to calm down. When she and her grandfather had discussed her part in this investigation, he'd warned her not to be contentious, to remember that Wade was in charge. Anyway, going with him wouldn't be such a hardship. She shrugged. "Oh, all right."

"Such enthusiasm." Wade gave her an amused look, then, as he glanced over her shoulder, his expression sobered. "Isn't that your ex-boyfriend?"

Sam turned to see Keith and a voluptuous blonde strolling across the lawn past the pool. Her hair was mussed, and Keith's tie was askew, his shirttail hanging out. They'd obviously been down to the bay for some serious petting. Keith's companion was hanging all over him, not that he seemed to mind. He stroked her bare arm and she stopped for a moment, stood on tiptoe and kissed his cheek. Keith glanced their way, then, as if performing for their benefit, he pulled

the woman into his arms for a long, and Sam thought, melo-
dramatic kiss.

From behind her, Wade asked, "Does that bother you?"

"No, you heard me tell Keith we were through. *He's* the one
who's bothered."

Wade put his hands on her shoulders and turned her to face
him. With a wicked gleam in his eye, he asked, "Shall we give
him something to worry about then?"

She'd always been reckless. No reason to quit now. "Why
not?"

"Here goes." He gripped the lapels of the jacket she was
wearing and tugged her closer. Sam put her hands lightly on
his shoulders.

She tipped her face up.

He bent his head. The blue eyes that met hers were filled
with laughter.

His lips touched hers lightly, flirting with them, teasing.
Backing away, then advancing.

Sam entered into the game, nibbling at Wade's lower lip,
teasing him back.

He trailed a line of tiny kisses along her jaw, then returned
to her mouth. "How am I doing?" he whispered, his breath
tickling her chin.

Sam laughed softly. "You're doing just fi—"

She didn't finish. Couldn't finish. The moment she opened
her mouth, his tongue dived inside and all she could manage
was a moan. A hoarse, longing sound from deep in her
throat. A sound that changed everything.

Wade's arms locked around her. He pulled her closer. His
breath rasped in her ear, his heart thudded against her
breasts. No more teasing, no more play. He kissed her for all
he was worth. Kissed her like nobody—no one in her life—
had ever kissed her.

4

SAM'S SENSES SWAM, her blood pounded in her ears. Wade's mouth plundered hers, possessed it. His hands held her captive. The jacket fell from her shoulders, but she didn't feel the cold, not with those hot hands roaming her back, those clever lips scorching her mouth.

She heard a whimpering sound. Hers. Then a groan. His.

She should pull away, tell him to stop, but she couldn't. She'd forgotten how to move, how to speak. She could only hang on to him for dear life and kiss him back.

From somewhere close by came the sound of voices, laughter, then footsteps coming nearer.

Wade's hands dropped from her shoulders. He took a step back.

Sam felt as if she were surfacing after a long, deep dive. She took a slow, shaky breath and stared at Wade. His sapphire eyes had turned to indigo. He looked as stunned as she felt.

Sam lifted a hand to her swollen lips. "I . . . we . . ."

Wade ran his fingers through his tousled hair. "I . . . didn't expect . . ."

"We need to think about this," Sam managed to whisper.

"Yeah," he muttered. He bent to pick up his jacket and shrugged into it. He cleared his throat. "Would you like a drink?"

Sipping a drink, smiling politely, making social conversation for the rest of the evening would be impossible. She felt as if a storm had ravaged her, stripping away everything she thought she knew and felt about herself. The cool, unflappable Samantha Brewster had disappeared, and in her place... She needed to think about that. "I'd like to go home."

"Okay. Let's take the outside stairs," he suggested, then grinned suddenly. "I imagine we both look like we've . . ."

Like we've come close to tearing each other's clothes off. Smoothing her hair, Sam turned toward the stairway.

Wade took her arm. Immediately, her body reacted. A fierce rush of desire surged through her. Oh, God, how could she work with him? Like Pavlov's dog, she was already conditioned to respond to him. And from only one kiss. But, regardless of her concerns, she didn't pull away.

Silently, they walked down the stairs and across the parking lot to Wade's car. The breeze cooled her heated cheeks. Now, if only something would restore her good sense.

On the drive home, Sam stared into the night. She'd always been a logical, goal-oriented person. She chose objectives and worked toward them. No deviations, no side trips.

Okay, this time she'd hit a small detour. She just needed to get back to the main road and she'd be on her way again. The thought made her feel better, and she relaxed.

When Wade walked her to her door, she unlocked it, then turned and met his eyes. "We're working together. We need to keep our minds on that." Damn it, her voice sounded uncertain. She lifted her chin and continued. "I'm going to forget what happened before."

"Are you now?" Wade's voice was soft. He stared down at her, his gaze piercing. "I'm not."

Before she could answer, he brushed a finger down her cheek, turned and walked away.

Sam shut the door behind her and leaned back against it. Heedless of her lace dress, she let herself slide down until she was sitting on the floor. She closed her eyes and let out a breath. "Oh, man!" From now on, working with Wade Phillips would be more of a challenge than she'd bargained for.

WADE PARKED in his garage, strode into the house and headed for his bedroom, shedding clothes as he went. He yanked off his black tie and dropped it on the entry-hall table, tossed his jacket on the living-room couch and stalked down the hall. In his bedroom he pitched his cummerbund in the direction of the dresser. With a sigh, he sat on the edge of the bed and began unbuttoning his shirt.

Had he warned Sam earlier that he was dangerous? He'd made a mistake. *She* was the one. *Dangerous* was too tame a word to describe her. Hell, the lady should come with a warning sign attached: Contents May Be Combustible.

They'd both nearly gone up in flames tonight. If they'd been somewhere private . . .

His mind conjured up the image—the delicious image—of Sam in his arms, the silver sheen of moonlight on her body, those little whimpering sounds coming from her throat. Just thinking about it, he felt like a volcano about to erupt.

"She's going to forget about it," he muttered. "Like hell!" Sam was no more going to forget their kiss than he was.

With a groan of unfulfilled desire, he flung the rest of his clothes in a heap on the floor, got out his running shoes and a pair of shorts and put them on. Slamming the front door behind him, he went out and jogged three miles.

SAM CURLED UP on her living-room couch and opened the book Tonya had left for her, *Murder By Fax,* the latest Nick Petrelli mystery. She and her cousin, both Petrelli fans, often traded the books. Sam liked nearly all private-eye stories, but this series was her favorite. "Based on the cases of a real private investigator." That made the stories so much more interesting. And she loved Nick Petrelli, the cowboy-detective. He was so Texan—casual, laid-back, but so sharp. And sexy. The man had a woman in every port . . . every book, actually. A date with Nick was just what she needed to get her mind off a certain real-life detective . . . whose only communication in five days had been impersonal notes by E-mail.

He'd apparently had an easier time forgetting the other night than he'd predicted. Just as well.

Sam glanced at the back cover of the mystery. She always hoped to find a photo of Paul Warden, but the enigmatic author of the Nick Petrelli series refused to have his picture on the book jacket or to make personal appearances. Probably it would interfere with his ability to work undercover.

Or maybe Paul Warden was the pseudonym of a woman. Paula Warden, perhaps. *There* was an interesting thought.

Maybe someday *she'd* write a book, Sam mused. Samantha Brewster. Let's see. She could be Samuel Bruce or Bruce Samson. *Not bad.*

She opened the book to chapter one and was soon engrossed, so absorbed that she considered ignoring the ringing of the phone. But she couldn't.

She picked it up. "Hello."

"Samantha." Wade's voice was smooth as silk.

Sam swallowed and squeezed her eyes shut. "Yes."

"You haven't forgotten that Garrett Franklin invited us to his party Friday night, have you?"

"No." Nothing that had happened between them had left her mind.

"I'll pick you up at eight." He paused, giving her time to envision and anticipate the evening to come. Then he said, "The Kitchen Table—that's Arnold Stewart's restaurant—is having a preopening party Saturday night. My friend at the *Express* wangled us an invitation. That should give us a chance to try out his chili."

"Fine."

"Find out anything about Helen Kay this week?" he asked.

"Not a thing," Sam admitted. And it wasn't as though she hadn't tried. "Helen is as closemouthed as a clam."

"Maybe we'll turn up something at the party."

The "we" pleased Sam. "Let's plan on it. Anything else you want me to do?"

He chuckled softly. "Nothing I can mention," he murmured, and she knew that whether he'd called in the past few days or not, he hadn't forgotten one iota of what had happened between them last week.

"I'll see you Friday," she said briskly. "Eight." She hung up and picked up her book, but suddenly Nick Petrelli's exploits didn't seem so exciting. Maybe some work would be good for her.

She tossed the book aside and went into her bedroom, where she sat at her desk and read over the list she'd been keeping of everything she and Wade knew about the missing recipe.

Reasons for entering a stolen recipe in a contest: no monetary gain but lots of prestige. Could be used in advertising. Could be basis for starting own chili company.

She needed to know more. Sam decided she'd investigate the chili cook-off world. Not only would that move them further along on the case, but she and Wade would have something to concentrate on besides each other on Friday night.

As soon as she reached her office the next morning, she began making calls. After only two, she was put in touch with CASI, the Chili Appreciation Society International. She called the president, Buck Stapleton. "I'm interested in learning about chili cook-offs," she began. "I have this old family recipe . . ."

"Well, little lady," he said, "you've come to the right place. Whereabouts d'ya live?"

Little lady! Sam gritted her teeth. "Houston."

"Texas!" Stapleton said. "You know the legislature there just named the jalapeño the state pepper."

She didn't know.

Stapleton continued jovially, "You wanna learn about chili, you just come on over to the Houston pod."

"The what?"

"The Houston pod. Our local chapter."

Oh, now she got it. Chili peppers—pod. Cute.

"Hold on a minute and I'll give you the number of the Great Pepper."

"Excuse me?"

"The Great Pepper. That's the president."

"Oh." If the president of the local organization was the Great Pepper, did that make Stapleton the Great Pepper of all Peppers?

In a moment, he returned and gave her the number. "They'll be happy to have you," he said. "I hope to meet you at one of our cook-offs. Good luck now, and may Chiligula be with you."

Chiligula? Confused, Sam blinked. But she called the Great Pepper, who turned out to be a friendly-sounding woman named Bonnie Marshall. She, too, invited Sam to attend the next pod meeting and offered to send her a copy of *Terlingua Trails*, CASI's newsletter. She, too, ended the conversation with, "May Chiligula be with you."

"Um, same to you." Sam hung up. Good Lord. Chiligula. The Great Pepper. Pods. She felt as if she'd left the known world and landed in Oz.

WADE LEANED an elbow against the bookcase, his casual stance belying his intense interest in the activity before him. Garrett Franklin's party was in full swing, high above Houston in the penthouse of one of the city's most prestigious apartment buildings. A sumptuous buffet was spread in the dining room, a state-of-the-art stereo provided music and the opulent rooms were filled with the Beautiful People of Houston.

In the space that had been cleared for dancing, a criminal attorney who had defended some of Texas's most well-heeled killers gyrated with an oil baron's wife. The oilman stood at the bar listening—or pretending to listen—while he ogled the cleavage of a young woman who'd just been elected to the state senate. Jake Merchant had cornered a prominent physician and was probably fishing for free medical advice. Jake's grandsons were absent this evening.

Before they'd arrived, Wade had told Sam to check out Franklin's apartment. Knowing the layout of the rooms never hurt. She'd asked Franklin for a tour, and they'd been gone a full fifteen minutes. Wade began to worry. If that lecher so much as laid a finger on Sam, Wade would have to break his bones.

Just then, Sam strolled into the living room with Franklin at her side. Wade snapped to attention, his gaze riveted to Franklin's hand on Samantha's arm. But several other guests waylaid them, and she slid out of Franklin's grasp.

Wade relaxed again and let his eyes rest on Sam. She was a pleasure to watch. Wearing a simple ice-blue dress with long sleeves, she looked far sexier than the overly made-up women cruising the room with their plunging necklines and iridescent gowns. There was something to be said for subtlety over blatant sexuality. A man could look at Sam and dream, wonder what it would be like to get beneath that regal surface and uncover the temptress waiting there.

"Well, well, if it isn't Nick Petrelli."

Wade almost dropped his glass. Had someone learned his secret?

He swung around and found himself staring into the mischievous brown eyes of Sam's cousin Tonya. No, she was teasing. He let out a relieved breath. Tonya didn't know how close she'd come to the truth.

"So, how's the great detective?" she asked. "Found the bad guys yet?"

"Nope."

"Is Sam any help?"

"Um . . ."

"Just what I thought. She's a pain in the—" she turned and set her glass down on the bookcase "—neck."

Wade laughed. "Yeah. Got any ideas on how to get her off this detective kick and onto something else?"

Tonya shook her head. "You won't change her mind. This isn't some spur-of-the-moment whim. It goes back a long way."

That surprised him. "Back to what?"

Tonya shrugged. "She'll tell you someday. When she trusts you enough."

Wade frowned. He searched for Sam in the crowd, but she'd disappeared. At least she wasn't with Franklin. The food magnate was standing in the corner, wooing the society columnist of one of Houston's major newspapers.

Tonya took Wade's drink, set it beside hers and tugged at his arm. "Come on. I've always wanted to dance with a detective."

Wade followed her to the dance floor. She was wearing a backless red minidress that left an amazing amount of honey-gold skin uncovered. With her sable hair and sparkling eyes, she drew the attention of most of the men in the room. If Wade had his choice, however, he'd rather look at Sam.

Tonya turned to him and began to move sinuously in time to the music. Wade joined her, keeping one eye on Garrett Franklin. He was still talking to the columnist, but now Helen Kay had joined them. Wade wondered what was going on between those two. He'd bet a year's worth of royalties it had something to do with the chili recipe.

The music stopped, and Tonya leaned toward him. Lowering her voice to a conspiratorial whisper, she asked, "Tell me, Wade, do you carry a weapon?"

He winked at her. "Yeah, but it's concealed."

Wade chuckled as Tonya's cheeks turned pink. Then Sam came back into the room and he couldn't take his eyes off her. She stood beneath a crystal chandelier. The light played over her hair, and it glowed like amber. She pushed a tendril behind her ear, and Wade watched, appreciating the grace with which she endowed the smallest movement. She glanced toward them and caught his eye. His heart began to thump.

Tonya followed his gaze. "Go ahead," she said. "You're dying to ask Sam to dance. Go on," she insisted when he hesitated. "See that blond guy in the horn-rimmed glasses over there? I've had my eye on him all evening." With a wave over her shoulder, she headed toward her prey. Wade watched her for a moment, then set out after his.

Sam watched Wade's approach. That confident stride, that sexy smile. That I-know-what-I-want-and-it's-you look in his blue eyes. Though she didn't change her expression, her insides turned to jelly.

He came up to her, leaned close. She could see the tiny silver flecks in his eyes. "Find out anything?" he murmured.

"Hmm? Oh," she said, forcing herself to pay attention to business. "No, nothing except that this apartment is *big*."

"Who's that talking to Jake Merchant over by the bar?"

Sam glanced across the room. "Uncle Ray."

"Donovan?" he asked sharply.

"Yes, but don't go getting worked up over it. They've known each other for a long time. They belong to the same golf club."

"Another rule, darlin'. Suspect *everyone*."

"Not Ray."

"Honey, the rest of that rule is . . . even your mother."

Sam gave him a disgusted look. "Right now, my money's on Helen. Look, there she goes with Garrett." They watched as their host left the room with the home economist.

"Why don't you wander after them and see what they're up to?" Wade suggested. "I'll head for the bar."

Sam sauntered out of the room and into the hall. Garrett and Helen were a few steps ahead of her. They turned into a bedroom, and she hurried after them, slipping into the room next to the one they'd entered. Good thing Wade had had her check out the apartment. She knew the two bedrooms were joined by a connecting bath.

Beneath the bathroom door, she saw a light. She heard water running. Sam stepped behind the bedroom curtains and waited. The curtains were dusty. She hoped she wouldn't sneeze.

She held her breath and heard the clink of a glass, then the water stopped. In a moment, the bathroom light went off, and she heard the door on the other side shut.

Sam tiptoed into the bathroom and put her ear to the door. Damn! Helen had said something, but her voice was too muffled for Sam to hear. She turned back to the counter and grabbed a glass. She'd always heard that you should put a glass up to the wall if you wanted to eavesdrop. She held the glass to the door and listened.

"Here you go," Garrett said. "Two aspirin."

Much better, Sam thought. His voice was still slightly muffled but it was louder.

"Thanks." Helen's voice. She moaned. "This headache's a bad one. I'm afraid I won't be able to stay late to talk."

"Let's get together another night," Garrett suggested. "How about Sunday?"

"Well, I have to—" Helen's next words were too faint for Sam to hear.

"Why don't I go with you and we'll talk afterward?" he said. "I'll pick you up at home."

"Fine. Seven o'clock."

Perfect, Sam told herself. She'd follow them, stick with them like glue for the entire evening and find out what they were up to. She waited for a few minutes after they left the bedroom, then strolled back to the living room, where Wade stood beside the bar, glass in hand.

"Buy you a drink?" he asked when she reached his side.

"Whatever you're having." She frowned. "I thought you told Granddad you don't drink on the job."

"I don't. This is ginger ale." He turned to the bartender and ordered one for her. "Let's go out on the balcony and talk," he suggested.

Sam followed him through the sliding door. She stood silently for a moment, enjoying the view. Houston spread out below them, its lights twinkling like sequins on a ball gown. "Beautiful," Sam said.

"Yeah." But he wasn't admiring the view. He was looking at her.

Sam took a step away and searched for something to shield her from his potent masculinity. A pot of chrysanthemums sat on a table behind her. She broke off a yellow flower and held it in front of her, twirling the stem between her fingers.

"I've been thinking," Wade began.

She kept her eyes on the chrysanthemum. "About what?"

"This." He plucked the flower from her hands and tossed it over the side of the balcony.

Some shield, she thought before his lips covered hers.

Where had he learned to kiss like that? He teased her lips apart, his tongue touched hers, caressed it, claimed it. "Wade," she moaned against his mouth. "Wade."

"Mmm?"

What had she wanted to say? "Helen," she muttered. "Helen and Garrett."

His hands dropped from her shoulders. "Damn, Samantha. You're messing up my mind. I forgot we were working." He smiled, a little-boy grin that couldn't disguise the fact that a man—a very aroused man—was standing before her. He stepped away and leaned against the railing. "What did they say?"

She waited a moment until the night breeze cooled her fevered body, then repeated the conversation she'd overheard.

Wade listened intently. "Sounds interesting. Ray and Jake may be up to something, too. They scheduled a golf game Sunday afternoon. Too bad I can't figure out a way to caddy for them."

"You wouldn't hear a thing from Uncle Ray," Sam said.

"Remember the rules, sweetheart. I'll have to bug his house and his phone."

Sam started to protest, then thought better of it. "And I'll follow Helen and Garrett."

"Correction. *We'll* follow them."

"*I* will."

"*We* will," Wade said.

Sam put her hands on her hips and glared at him.

"Damn it, Sam," Wade muttered. "You are the most irritating female. If I weren't a gentleman, I'd be tempted to throttle you."

"Go ahead and try," she challenged. When he didn't move, she smiled triumphantly. She'd won that point. "Somehow," she said under her breath, "I'd gotten the feeling you really weren't a gentleman."

"We'll discuss that later. Right now we have company." He nodded toward the sliding door.

Two women came out on the balcony, one of them Mitzi Edgar, the society columnist for the Houston *Express*. Sam tried to slip past them, but Mitzi put a hand on her arm. She peered at Sam in the dim light. "You're Clint Brewster's granddaughter, aren't you?"

Sam stiffened. "Yes."

"Your name?"

The last thing Sam wanted was her name in the paper. She scrambled for a way to get out of the situation gracefully, then decided to be direct. "If you're asking for your column, I'd rather not tell you."

Mitzi looked surprised. "Publicity-shy, hmm? You're one of the few. Okay, you won't see it in print."

Sam didn't believe Mitzi for a moment. "Thanks. I'm—" What had Drew called her the other evening? "Serena." She saw Wade's surprised reaction but ignored him.

"How do you do, Serena," Mitzi said. "I hope you'll read my column." She grinned charmingly. "Just to be sure your name isn't in it."

"I'll do that. Nice meeting you."

She and Wade went inside. "Since when did you become Serena?" he asked.

"Since that woman wanted to put my name in the paper. You heard me tell her how I feel about publicity." She sighed. "Mitzi can find out my real name if she wants to, but this'll slow her down, maybe even make her think."

Several acquaintances of Sam's cornered them as soon as they returned to the living room, and they had no further chance to talk privately until the party ended and they were in Wade's car. They argued all the way home about who was going to do what and were still at an impasse when Wade turned into the driveway on the Brewster estate.

"You'll botch it," he grumbled. "You've had zero experience in tailing someone."

"That's as much as *you* had when you started," Sam said. "I believe in learning by doing."

"Be sensible," he argued. "You don't know what Garrett and Helen are up to. You may not get close enough to hear anything."

"If I can't, then neither could you," Sam told him, crossing her arms over her chest.

"I can get closer than you. They know you. They'd notice you in a minute."

Sam was tempted to point out that Helen had met Wade. Not only that, Helen, or any woman with breath in her body, would notice him, but Sam kept quiet. He probably knew that already. Instead, she said, "It's a waste of time and talent for both of us to do a job that's only big enough for one."

"So stay home." He pulled up before the guest house, got out of the car and slammed the door.

Sam didn't wait for him to come around. She got out, too. Wade was fast, though. He caught her arm as she started toward the door. "Sam, I'll give you three choices. I go, we both go or no one goes."

"Unfair choices."

"I'm in charge here, so I'm setting the rules."

Frustrated, she stopped in the doorway and glared at him. "I don't like your rules."

"Tough." He took her by the shoulders. In the light over the door, she could see that his eyes were dark, intense. "I don't want anything to happen to you."

"Nothing will happen." She bit out the words.

"I won't take that chance."

"Leave me alone, Wade." Furious now, she lifted her fists to shove at his chest.

He pulled her against him. "I can't, damn it." His voice deepened. "I can't."

She had an instant before he kissed her. She had the time to gather her strength and twist out of his arms. But her body seemed to have a will of its own. Her lips were already parting, her arms twining around his neck. With only the faintest feeling of regret, she gave herself up to his kiss.

He wasn't gentle this time. His kiss was hot, demanding, breath-robbing. He stole her breath, her thoughts, good Lord, her common sense. When he finally let her go, she felt as if he'd left his brand on her. "I'll pick you up at six tomorrow," he said.

Dumbly, she stared at him, wondering how his voice could be so steady.

"For the Kitchen Table."

She gasped. "The what?"

"Arnold Stewart's restaurant. Wear jeans." He turned and walked away.

Sam let out a choked laugh. When he'd said "kitchen table" after that searing kiss, her thoughts had conjured up quite a different picture. Not a café, but a vivid image of herself and Wade, naked, tangled together on her kitchen table.

She went inside and slammed the door, wondering if that fantasy would come true.

WHEN SAM WOKE the next morning, her fingers flew to her lips. She could almost feel the imprint of Wade's kisses. Her mind was still full of him. She hadn't intended for this to happen, yet she couldn't deny the attraction she felt for him. She wasn't one to hop into bed with a man just because of chemistry—though she couldn't remember the chemistry being quite so powerful before. She had to care about someone, respect him. Of course, she respected Wade's investigative skills, but that didn't earn him an invitation to her bed. Damn it, she'd wanted a mentor, not a lover. Why did life have to be so complicated?

Throughout the day, though she tried to put Wade out of her mind, he lurked there, popping into her thoughts at odd times. She passed a Western store and remembered the way Wade's jeans molded his thighs . . . and the way those thighs had felt pressed against hers. She heard a love song on her car radio and remembered Wade's kiss. Even the warm scent of the garden surrounding her house evoked his essence. She'd better watch herself tonight, or she'd succumb to his charms without a second thought.

As six o'clock approached, she found herself pacing nervously, wondering what would happen between her and Wade this evening. Damn, she was a woman who was never nervous. What was it about this man? How should she handle him? She'd be cool, she promised herself. Minimally friendly, but indifferent.

But when Wade arrived at six sharp, looking as if he'd ridden out of the Old West in his faded jeans and Western shirt, she forgot her good intentions. How could she be indifferent when the man had the audacity to pull her into his arms and kiss her the minute she opened the door?

Clearly, some sort of response was called for here. Sam cleared her throat. "I think we should put our attraction aside for the moment, while we're working together." She'd rehearsed this speech while she was in the tub in case something happened that called for it. The kiss just now called for it. The speech had sounded good earlier. "We both agreed we need time to think."

"Time to think. Okay."

"We're agreed then?"

"Agreed," he said amiably. Too amiably?

Sam eyed him warily as they drove to the Kitchen Table, but he behaved impeccably. Even when he took her arm to lead her to the door of the restaurant, his touch was that of a colleague or acquaintance. Sam decided she could relax.

Well, semi-relax. If she'd learned one fact about Wade Phillips in the short time she'd known him, it was that he was anything but predictable.

At the entrance of the café, Arnold Stewart's partners greeted guests. As befitted a silent partner, Arnold stayed inside in the background; yet he looked authentic in a plaid shirt with sleeves rolled up, jeans and a belt with a gigantic silver buckle.

The Kitchen Table was about as down-home as you could get. Front porch with wooden slats and a wooden railing that looked as if it had come straight off the tree. Red-and-white-checked tablecloths. Waitresses in denim skirts and fringed shirts scurrying around with big pitchers of beer or iced tea. A jukebox blaring country-western tunes, and signs for horse liniment, chewing tobacco and cornmeal on the walls. The menu featured meat loaf, chicken-fried steak with cream gravy, and, of course, several varieties of Texas chili.

"We'll have one order of each kind of chili," Wade told the waitress.

Her eyes widened. "Wow, y'all must really like chili."

"Love it." When the woman dashed off, he turned to Sam. "We'll taste them all and take the rest home for your grandfather. He'll be back tomorrow, won't he?"

Sam nodded. As they headed for the salad bar, she glanced around the restaurant, hunting for familiar faces.

Wade, too, scanned the crowd. Sam noticed him eyeing a tall brunette wearing designer jeans, a suede jacket and a silver-and-turquoise necklace that looked so heavy, Sam bet the woman would need a neck brace tomorrow. The woman eyed him back. Who was she? Sam wondered. An old flame? A current girlfriend? And why on earth did she care?

Sam had no chance to ask about the woman, because Drew Merchant cornered them. "Hello, Sabrina," he said.

"Samantha."

He shrugged. "What are you doing here? Don't you get enough chili at your granddad's?"

"Just checking out the competition," Sam said. "What about you?"

Drew's smile was sly. "Same thing."

When Drew swaggered off, Sam turned to Wade, who was busy filling his salad plate. "What do you think that meant?"

"Maybe Tru-Tex has your grandfather's recipe, maybe not."

"Oh, that's helpful," Sam sniffed as she added dressing to her salad. Between the memory of Wade's kisses and the sight of that brunette's eyes boring into him, she was on edge and found it easy to get annoyed.

He ignored her sarcasm and nodded to their table. "Our order's there. Let's go try our chili."

They spent half an hour tasting, comparing and tasting again. Wade dubbed the three dishes hot, hotter and hottest. "Any of 'em taste like Clint's?" he asked.

"Maybe the second, but I can't be sure. He'll know."

Wade signaled the waitress and asked for carry-home containers.

Sam excused herself and went to the ladies' room.

The lounge was decorated in gingham and ruffles. Sam sat at the old-fashioned dressing table and freshened her lipstick. When she finished, she put her makeup back in her purse, then looked up and met the eyes of the woman Wade had been staring at earlier.

"Hello," the brunette drawled. "I saw you with Wade."

"Yes."

"He and I are old friends." The woman smiled and extended a ring-bedecked hand. "I'm Marlene McKenna, formerly Phillips, Wade's ex-wife."

Sam admonished herself for the feeling of relief that swept through her. Why should she feel that way? She and Wade were collaborating, not cohabiting, for goodness' sake. "Sam Brewster," she said.

"So, are you and Wade seeing each other?"

"In a way." What way was none of Marlene's business.

"Are you his latest heroine? Or the one who done it?"

Sam stared at the woman in confusion. "I don't know what you're talking about."

"Wade's alter ego."

When Sam said nothing, only frowned, Marlene laughed. "I guess I let the cat out of the bag. Sorry," she added, looking decidedly unapologetic. "Well, since I've mentioned it, I'd better explain."

She sat down, and Sam waited impatiently while Marlene opened her denim bag and dumped a tube of lipstick, a mascara brush, eye shadow and an eyelash curler onto the counter. What on earth did she intend to reveal about Wade? Was he an ex-con? A recovering drug addict? A CIA agent?

Marlene applied lipstick, blotted, then reached for the eye shadow. "In his other life, he's Paul Warden."

Sam dropped her purse. "Paul Warden? Y-you mean, he's the . . . author?"

Marlene paused with the mascara wand poised and nodded. "The very one. Nick Petrelli's creator, the reclusive mystery writer." Her eyes swept over Sam. "Watch for yourself in his next story."

"Oh, he wouldn't—"

Marlene chuckled. "He would. It's a given." She stashed her makeup in her purse and stood. "Nice meeting you, Sam. Tell Wade I said hello."

Sam watched in the mirror as Marlene sauntered out of the lounge. Of all the things Wade's ex might have told her, this was the very last one she'd expected.

Wade Phillips. Just turn the initials around and you got Paul Warden. Now that she knew, it made sense. So did the BMW, the designer tux.

Nick Petrelli, she thought. *Oh, my God. Nick Petrelli.* His cases were based on the files of a real private investigator. Did that mean the missing chili recipe was about to become the subject of a Nick Petrelli mystery? *Over my dead body.*

Sam swallowed as an even more disturbing thought occurred to her. Was *she* about to become the subject of a Nick Petrelli story? One of Nick's string of love-'em-and-leave-'em affairs? Were those hot kisses she and Wade had shared research for his next novel?

He'd better not bet his next advance check on it! Jumping up, she grabbed her purse and marched out of the room.

5

WADE SAT at the table, sipping ginger ale and watching the crowd. He noticed Arnold Stewart coming out of the kitchen, Drew Merchant charming one of the waitresses. He wondered if either of them was the chili thief. Stewart seemed too smart, Merchant was a question mark. He was sharper than his brother, which was like comparing a frog to a toad, but he had too big a mouth to be a successful thief.

Once Sam's grandfather returned from London and tasted Stewart's chili, they'd have a pretty good idea if the restaurateur had stolen the recipe. Wade sighed. If Stewart turned out to be the culprit, the case would be closed and his reason for seeing Sam would be over. But he didn't intend to let that happen. Nope, case or not, he planned on seeing a great deal more of Ms. Brewster.

She came out of the rest room and walked gracefully across the dining room. Even in jeans and Western shirt, with her hair in a simple braid, she looked like a princess. As he watched her, his body reacted in all the right places.

He smiled as she came up to the table and he reached for her hand. "Well, darlin'—"

She stepped back. "Has the waitress brought our check?"

"Uh-uh. I thought you might want some dessert."

"No, thank you." She took her seat and signaled the waitress. The imperious gesture made her look more like a queen than a mere princess.

The waitress appeared, carrying the plastic take-out cartons. "How 'bout some cobbler or a piece of pie?" the woman said.

"No, thank you," Sam said and folded her hands. "Just the check, please." She looked cool and aloof. But her eyes blazed.

"Want to tell me what's eating you?" Wade asked when the waitress walked away. "You're madder than a cat with its tail in a vise."

Sam looked down her aristocratic nose at him. "We'll discuss it in the car."

"Okay," he said and eyed her with interest. He'd seen her frustrated, annoyed, even angry. But this time, she was enraged. When this woman got really mad, she turned to ice.

The waitress returned, he took care of the bill, picked up the take-out containers and followed Sam outside. He watched her curiously. She stood as still as a statue, waiting for the parking attendant to bring the car.

When they were in the car, Wade said, "All right, now tell me what's got you all bent out of shape."

She studied his face as if he were some particularly unpleasant species of insect, then said, "Paul Warden."

Wade felt as if she'd punched him in the gut. "Uh-oh. Let me guess. You had a talk with Marlene."

"Right."

With a screech of brakes, he pulled out of the parking lot and swung into the street. Damn his ex-wife. She wasn't supposed to blab this information around and she knew it. *He'd* have a talk with her. Soon. "What's wrong?" he said. "Are you angry because I didn't tell you myself?"

"Since it could affect our business association, yes. If we had a personal relationship, I might feel differently."

After the kisses they'd exchanged, he could argue with her definition of their relationship, but he let it pass. "Tell me how you think my writing affects our business together," he said.

"Are you writing a book about the chili recipe?"

"Yes and no."

"Be a little more specific." Without raising her voice a decibel, she managed to convey enough frosty disdain to lower the temperature in the car a good twenty degrees. Nevertheless, heat flared in her eyes.

A man had to beware of a woman like that, Wade thought. He'd never know if he was in danger of being swallowed by a glacier or scorched by the volcano boiling beneath it. "I base my books on real life," he said. "I don't duplicate it."

"Meaning?"

"Real life's too predictable, a lot of it's too boring. The germ of an idea comes from my cases, but I twist it, color it, give it my own slant. You'll never recognize your granddad or his company in my book."

"I see." She stared out the window, her features as composed as if they'd been exchanging information about the weather. Then, her voice even quieter, she said, "Am I in the book?"

Hell's bells, he wouldn't just talk to Marlene. He'd murder her . . . slowly and with great pleasure. "Now, Sam," he said in a placating tone as he thought of Al McGuire, the beauteous detective Nick was collaborating with. "You're overreacting here—"

"Answer the question."

"No one would identify you."

"*I* would."

He'd change Al's hair color, make her ugly . . .

"I want to read the manuscript," Samantha said.

"No." He braked at a stoplight and glanced at her.

"Yes."

"No," he repeated. "No way."

"Why not?"

"No one reads my work until it's on the shelves. That's a rule."

"What kind of rule?" Her voice sounded haughtier than ever. "One of the Ten Commandments?"

"Right," he said. "Thou shalt not show a first draft to anyone."

She let out a ragged sigh. "All right, don't violate your rule, but listen to me. I . . . don't . . . want . . . to be in your book." She leaned toward him. In the light from the street lamps, he saw that her eyes were dark, serious.

She wasn't angry now, Wade realized, she was apprehensive. He remembered her remark to the gossip columnist about not wanting her name in the newspaper, and he gave in. "Okay." He'd never let *anyone*'s whims dictate his work before, but this was different. Sam was important to him. "I have a woman in the book," he said, "but she won't be you." He would have to do a lot more rewriting than he had time for, but he'd doctor up Al McGuire so that she played the role he intended for her, but she wouldn't be a detective, she wouldn't be rich or blond. But he refused to give up sexy. Nick deserved that much. He crossed the intersection, then glanced at Sam. "Satisfied?"

"I don't seem to have a choice," she said, looking none too happy.

He touched her hand. "You can trust me."

"We'll see." *You'll have to convince me*, her tone said. She settled back and stared thoughtfully at him. "You're the last person I'd expect to be a writer."

"Why?" he asked, not sure her remark pleased him. "Because I'm not wild-eyed and gaunt, with long hair? Because I drive a nice car and don't live in a garret?"

Sam shook her head. "You're not introspective enough."

"I'm analytical. That's what it takes to write mysteries."

"I like your books," she said, flashing a sudden smile that nearly stopped his breath. "The one about the librarian who laundered money and hid it in the literary classics is my favorite."

Her remark pleased him more than he wanted to let on. "Thanks," he drawled, inclining his head. "Always glad to hear from a fan."

"Was that story about a real case?" she asked, evidently still concerned about appearing in the current book.

"Yeah," he said, "but the money launderer was a bookstore owner, not a librarian, and, appropriately enough, she hid the cash in books on economics. I caught her when she got to *The Wealth of Nations*."

"What about Nick?" she asked. "Is he you?"

"Pretty much. Of course, some of the things that happen to Nick are fictitious, but his thoughts and feelings and his philosophy of life—those are all mine."

"How'd you get into writing?" Sam asked.

"You want my life story, darlin'?" She nodded and he said, "I started out to be a lawyer."

Sam digested this. "What happened?"

"My dad died my first year in law school. He'd taken out a big loan two years before and finances got tight. I took a job with a private investigator to help pay my way through school."

"Is that when you changed your mind?"

Wade shook his head. "I graduated from law school and got a job with Hartley, Wayne and Dreyfuss."

She raised an eyebrow. "Fancy firm."

"Yeah, Marlene was ecstatic. She'd worked, too, when I was in law school, and she saw her investment paying off big-time."

"And then?"

"And then one of those little things happened that can change your life. I was sitting in the dentist's office, waiting to have a tooth filled, and I picked up a magazine—*Crime Scene*—and started leafing through it. They were having a contest for the best short story, and for the heck of it, I entered."

"Had you always wanted to write?"

He laughed. "Never. I was a reporter on my high-school paper and I made good grades in English composition, but writing was something for intellectuals and I didn't figure that was me. But I entered a story based on one of the cases I'd worked on with the P.I. and won two thousand dollars. A couple of weeks after the magazine published my story, I got a letter from an agent named Harold Borden. He said I had talent and if I ever decided to go into mystery writing seriously, to look him up."

"Did you?"

"Not then. I played around with writing, though, and pretty soon I was hooked. I started spending more and more time on it. You can't do that and make the grade with a law firm. They run on slave hours. I'd work all day and write half the night. And then I began thinking more about my story than my next case. Finally, I said to hell with law, quit the firm and went back to working for the private eye. I called Harold Borden and a year later I had my first book contract."

"And Marlene?"

"She didn't stay around for the sale. Marlene was outa there in six months. Her aspirations were higher than being the wife of a detective and wanna-be writer." He didn't often dwell on his marriage—after all, six years had passed since the divorce, and the breakup had long since ceased to matter to him—but talking about it reminded him how much better off he was alone.

Sam laid her hand on his arm. "Marlene's aspirations were too low," she said.

A sudden, unexpected lump welling in his throat, Wade put his fingers over hers and squeezed. "Thanks."

Gently, Sam removed her hand. "I guess your divorce made you negative about women and marriage."

"Nah, not about women," he said with a half smile. "Just marriage." He stopped at another red light and glanced at Sam to gauge her reaction. His sentiments turned off some women, but he felt he had to be honest.

"I guess," she said, "as long as a woman knows where she stands from the start . . ."

"From the start," he repeated softly. "Are you talking about you and me, darlin'? Is this the start for us?"

They stared at each other in silence. Her scent flowed over him, spicy and alluring. Longing surged through him, heady and sharp. *Say yes*, he thought, his mind reaching out to her. He wanted to pull her into his arms, right here in the middle of the street, and the hell with traffic.

Her lips curved ever so slightly. "Maybe. But we need to take it slow."

That wasn't the answer he wanted, but it was better than "no." A horn honked behind him, and Wade pressed down on the accelerator. "You've read my books. You know I believe in fast starts."

"Ah, but you said a while ago that fiction doesn't duplicate real life." She inched closer to the door and changed the subject. "So, Paul," she said, using his pen name. "Will you autograph some books for me?"

"Sure, as long as you don't spread it around that I'm the author."

Sam's lips curved into a teasing smile. "I won't breathe a word . . . unless you give me reason to consider blackmail." She spoke in a low, sultry tone that gave him goose bumps.

"I'd never do that, darlin'."

"Then I'll just feel superior because I know the answer to 'The Secret of Paul Warden.'"

"You must've seen that article in *Newsweek* a couple of months ago," he said with a grimace.

"I did, and I think keeping your identity secret is great. Staying anonymous adds to your mystique. Your fans can imagine you any way they like."

"How did you imagine me?"

Sam gave him a sly smile. "Oh, blond, British, wearing a tweed jacket and horn-rimmed glasses, smoking a pipe."

"Liar."

"Yeah." She chuckled. "Actually, I wasn't far off from the real you."

"Hah," he said. "A rakish charmer."

"I'll take the Fifth on that," Sam said.

Wade smiled. He was surprised to see that they were only a few blocks from Sam's. He didn't want the evening to end, especially not after their exchange a few minutes ago. "Would you like to—"

The pager at his belt shrilled.

"Damn!" He checked the readout and grabbed his cellular phone. "It's a client." He punched in the number of Don Juanito's wife. "Yes, Carole, this is Wade." He listened to Carole McKenzie's desperate voice and said, "Another call? Okay, I'll be over in ten minutes. I'll stay there tonight and arrange for a bodyguard tomorrow. Meantime, don't open the door to anyone else, even if you know them."

He turned down the Brewsters' street. "Sorry."

"It's okay."

Not with him. He wanted to spend the rest of the evening with Sam, listening to her voice, learning more about her, touching her. Especially touching her. He wanted them mouth to mouth, body to body.

He pulled up to her door and, reluctantly, got back to business. "About tomorrow. I should be finished at Ray's by six, then I'll come over. Wait for me. We'll follow Helen and Garrett together."

She didn't answer.

He got out of the car, walked around and opened her door. "Sam," he prodded.

Still no answer.

He groaned with frustration. "I want you to hold off until I get here. Don't do anything stupid."

"I never do anything stupid." The haughty princess again.

"I'm tempted to handcuff you to the bed, but I guess I'll have to trust you."

He took her wrist as he walked her to the door and felt her pulse beneath his fingers. Not fast enough. He wanted to make it race. A soft breeze stirred the trees and brought the fragrance of late-summer roses. Or was it Samantha's scent? Half-drunk with desire, he kissed her . . . hard. So hard that when he pulled away, they both were trembling.

He had to leave. Hesitantly, he took a step away, then pivoted and pulled her close for one last, quick kiss. "Night, Samantha," he said. "I'll see you tomorrow."

He made it to the car, though his head was still reeling from her kisses. He sat for a moment, getting his breath. Sam aroused his temper, his protective instincts and his hormones, all at the same time. He wanted to forget about his client, pound on Sam's door, sweep her up in his arms and carry her to bed. He wanted to watch her eyes heat with desire, see her body flush with passion and know it was for him. He wanted to make love to her until they were both out of their minds. He was out of his mind already. No woman had ever made him feel like this.

He liked women. He'd had his share. If that was all he wanted—just a woman—there were plenty who'd be happy to accommodate him. Even Carole McKenzie, his client, had let him know she wasn't averse to mixing a little pleasure with their business. Don Juanito had gone out of town this weekend, and Carole's bed was there for the sharing. But he didn't want Carole McKenzie. He didn't want just a woman. He wanted Sam.

What attracted him? That regal, touch-me-not air? The passion he knew lurked below her cool surface? Her determination, her spirit? All of them combined.

He shifted uncomfortably in the seat. The night ahead promised to be long and lonely.

LATE THE NEXT AFTERNOON, Wade slipped out of Ray Donovan's house and shut the door gently. He crossed the backyard, crept through the ligustrum hedge and into the alley. He'd bugged Ray's phone, planted a listening device in his study, then he'd spent an hour going through the man's files. *Nada.* Nothing even slightly suspicious. Sam might be right—Ray Donovan could just be Clint Brewster's loyal employee and friend who also happened to enjoy playing golf with a competitor.

Wade got into his car and glanced at the clock on the dashboard. Damn, it was nearly six-thirty. He punched in Sam's number on his car phone.

The answering machine picked up.

He called her car and got the damn out-of-the-service-area message again. Like the other night. Hadn't she remembered to replace the darn battery?

When he got to Sam's, she was gone. He felt a flash of anger first, then one of fear. Damn her, she'd gone out after Garrett and Helen alone. "Idiot!" he snarled. He *should* have handcuffed her to the bed. He'd thought all day about making love to Sam, had even slipped a condom into his pocket.

Now he clenched his teeth. When he got hold of Sam, he wouldn't take her to bed; he'd throttle her.

He called directory assistance and got Helen Kay's address. Thank God, Helen's phone number was listed, so the address was available. He shot out of the Brewsters' driveway and headed for the suburb of West University, a thirty-minute drive. With sparse Sunday traffic and a little bit of luck, he could make it there in fifteen.

He heard the siren as he sped down Memorial Drive, then he saw the flashing light. "Oh, hell!"

The officer who waved him over did not look friendly. He was burly and red-faced and moved slower than a lame turtle. Unsnapping his holster, the policeman strolled over to the BMW as if he had all the time in the world. When he reached the car, he scowled at Wade and drawled, "Where ya headed, pal?"

To the hospital. I'm in labor. No, the guy didn't look as if he had a sense of humor. "To pick up a friend."

"You were doing sixty in a thirty-five-mile zone."

"Uh, sorry." *Now write the ticket and get it over with.*

"I'll have to see your driver's license."

Wade already had it out.

The policeman scrutinized it thoroughly, glancing up every now and then to compare Wade with the picture, in which he looked like an escaped con. "I'll have to write you a ticket." He proceeded to do so—in slow motion—then he delivered a lecture on the evils of speeding, while Wade gritted his teeth and clenched his fists around the steering wheel.

When the officer finally waved him on, Wade knew that unless Garrett was late to pick up Helen, he would miss them.

He did. Probably by ten minutes, the exact amount of time he'd spent with the representative of Houston's finest.

He decided to go back to Sam's and wait until she returned from following Garrett and Helen. He hoped Helen Kay wasn't a late-night person.

He retraced his route—at a sedate speed this time—and parked in front of Sam's door. Reaching into the glove compartment, he extracted a book on corporate spying and forced himself to read.

But a nagging feeling of uneasiness interfered with his concentration. He told himself Sam was on routine surveillance, but that didn't calm his fears. She was alone, unprotected. What if Garrett saw her? What if there was trouble? The what ifs multiplied and played havoc with his nerves. An hour went by and he hadn't read more than two pages. Ten more minutes passed, then his pager went off. Wade nearly shot out of the seat. Hands shaking, he yanked the small black box from his pocket. Carole McKenzie's number again.

The bodyguard answered. "I caught a fellow trying to sneak in through the patio door," he said. "Thought I'd let you know before I called the police."

"Good thinking," Wade said. "Hold off on the cops. I'll be right over."

He'd question the guy, then return to Sam's. Surely by the time he got back, she'd be home.

SAM HUNG BACK in the shadows as Garrett and Helen entered the three-story brick building on South Main near downtown Houston. The front of the building had no sign, only a street number. It seemed to be an office building of some sort, but it certainly wasn't Garrett's personal office. His company was located in one of the skyscrapers in the high-rent district in the middle of the city.

She looked around to see if anyone else was in the vicinity, but the street was deserted, so she walked quickly to the entrance and jiggled the doorknob. The building wasn't locked.

She slipped inside and found herself in an old theater. From her childhood, she vaguely remembered one of the forerunners of Theater Under the Stars around this neighborhood. She glanced at the building directory as she passed the elevator and noticed that the two upper floors housed various offices—an apartment locator, an accounting firm and several others.

She tiptoed across the silent lobby, opened the door a crack and peeped into the auditorium. It was dark, musty and nearly empty. The stage was lit, though, and people were walking around with scripts in their hands, placing chairs and making chalk marks on the floor.

Sam ducked inside and took the far corner seat in the last row. When her eyes got used to the dim light, she saw that Garrett was seated near the front. Why was he here, and where was Helen?

She waited. After a while, a tall, bushy-haired man strode in from the wings. "We'll read through act one," he announced in deep, stentorian tones. This was the rehearsal of a play, and he, apparently, was the director. He looked the part, in a black turtleneck and worn jeans. He perched on the edge of the stage, script and pen in hand.

Cast members assembled and took their positions. Sam was astonished to see Helen among them. She would never have figured the home economist for an actress. A church organist maybe, but an aspiring thespian, never. Maybe she had a walk-on part.

The rehearsal began.

Surprisingly, Helen had a major role and read her part with skill and emotion. She played Eve, a middle-aged woman, physically exhausted and financially drained from nursing her sister through a terminal illness. Loretta, the sister, had been the mistress of a senator who was now considering a run for the presidency. Several years before her death, she had written her memoirs. Eve—Helen—was contemplating selling the memoirs to a publisher.

"Loretta's illness cost me everything I had. I need cash. Who else can I turn to?"

Up to now, Sam had found the play riveting, but the last line sounded like something she'd heard before, like something she would have heard on a soap opera. But she didn't watch soap operas.

"I have nothing to sustain me but my pride," Helen continued. "Soon even that will be gone."

Sam gasped. She hadn't heard those words before, she'd read them . . .

Oh, God, she'd read them on Helen's computer disk!

Helen hadn't been writing about stealing the chili recipe. She'd been reprising her character in the play.

A feeling of triumph swelled in Sam's chest. She'd made an important discovery in the case, and she'd done it herself. Wade's own fault, too. If he'd showed up on time, he'd have been in on this. She'd kept her word and waited for him, then when he hadn't arrived by six-thirty, she'd taken off alone. As well she should! There was absolutely no reason for him to tag along. Let him spy on Uncle Ray. He'd learn nothing there because there was nothing to learn. She, on the other hand, had discovered what Helen's cryptic notes meant. She'd made headway!

But that still didn't explain Helen's relationship with Garrett Franklin. Sam decided to stay and try to find out more.

She sat through the rehearsal and waited as the theater emptied. Helen came down from the stage and spoke to Garrett, then the two of them headed backstage. Sam followed.

She stood hidden behind the side curtain of the darkened stage and tried to hear their conversation. They were too far away.

Carefully, quietly, Sam inched closer, pressing against the wall. Garrett and Helen disappeared around a corner. When they returned, would they notice her? How would she explain herself if they did? She held her breath.

"My purse is in the dressing room," Helen said. "I'll be right out."

Footsteps sounded, a door opened and shut, and Sam heard Garrett's voice. "Your theater group is good."

"Thanks."

Sam edged forward. The floor creaked.

"Did you hear something?" Helen asked.

"These old buildings are always rattling," Garrett said. "I'll take a look."

Sam stood, horrified, as steps came in her direction. She was about to race behind the curtain, when she saw a door. She jerked it open, lunged in and pulled the door shut behind her.

She'd stepped into a small, dark closet. From the smell of bleach and detergent, she guessed it contained janitorial supplies. She prayed Garrett hadn't heard the click of the door and tried to keep her teeth from chattering.

Heavy footsteps stopped inches from Sam's hiding place. "It was nothing," Garrett called.

Lighter steps sounded. "This is a wonderful old building," Helen said in a gushy voice Sam had never heard from her before. "You were so kind to let us use it for this play. It's an important presentation for the group."

"Glad to help you out," Garrett said.

Helen sighed dramatically. "We badly need a building. I wish I could persuade you to donate the space permanently. Wouldn't your doing that constitute a sizable tax deduction?"

Garrett chuckled. "It might, but that's not enough."

Their voices became fainter. Sam strained to hear.

"What would it take to convince you?" Helen asked.

"I'd have to get something in return."

Helen said something, but they were too far away for Sam to catch it. They must be on their way out. Surely she could follow them now. She twisted the doorknob. Nothing happened.

Irritated, she turned it harder. Again, nothing.

Sam's heart dropped to her toes. The lock must be backward, which meant that the door locked from the other side.

She was trapped.

6

"No!" Sam told herself. "There's no reason to panic." The door was just stuck. One good shove and it would open.

She leaned against it, pushed it, rattled it, to no avail. It didn't move a millimeter.

Was anyone left in the building?

She pounded on the door and shouted for help. She even seized a mop and banged the handle on the ceiling. She didn't care who rescued her—Garrett, Helen, anyone—or what they thought of her being on the premises. She just wanted out.

No one came.

"Calm down," Sam ordered herself. "Think." Her penlight, she remembered, was in her pocket. She dug it out and pressed the button. Slowly she turned, aiming the tiny light on the shelves behind her. Maybe she could find a hammer or some other tool to break the lock. She could find nothing useful, only bottles of cleanser and disinfectant, cans of floor wax and other things she couldn't make out. She trained the light on the door, then fumbled in her purse, hoping to find something sharp to insert in the keyhole and spring the latch. Her fingers closed over a ballpoint pen. She shoved it into the hole and twisted, but nothing happened.

The closet was cramped, the smell of bleach overpowering. She had no room to move, not even enough space to sit comfortably. The shelves pressed against her back. She heard a tiny rustling sound at her feet and barely suppressed a scream. Was it a cockroach? Or something worse? She shivered and shrank back against the shelves.

Why hadn't she waited for Wade? Why hadn't she brought her cellular phone with her? No one knew where she was. She could starve in here or suffocate. Months later, they'd find her bones on the closet floor. She bit back a sob and tried to stifle her panic.

But she couldn't. Old remembered fears surfaced, and suddenly she was eleven again. The year she and her sister had been kidnapped.

It had happened on a dark, moonless night. Their parents had been out for the evening, the sitter downstairs, and she and eight-year-old Susan already asleep. Sam had abruptly awakened to see two men in ski masks standing by her bed. One of them pinioned Susan with his arms, holding her still. Her sister's eyes were wild with fear.

The other man put his hand over Sam's mouth. "Don't make a sound," he warned her in a harsh whisper. He gagged and blindfolded her and dragged her roughly out of bed. He pushed her ahead of him down the back stairs, then slung her over his shoulder and carried her across the lawn. He put her down somewhere hard and uncomfortable. She heard a thump. The other man must have dumped Susan next to her.

Sam kicked out wildly and guessed she connected with her captor because she heard a grunt. But she hadn't hurt him enough because he tied her arms and legs, then she heard a slam and a minute later felt the vibration of an engine. They were in the trunk of a car, Sam realized. She couldn't see or move. She could only smell motor oil, feel the bumpiness of the ride and the chills racking her body. Her terror of the dark, airless prison and what might come later threatened to choke her, but she fought the fear, forcing herself to breathe.

If she was frightened, she knew Susan was petrified. Sam made a sound in her throat to let her younger sister know she was beside her, and Susan moaned. Sam made another sound, a hum, trying to calm her sister, but Susan continued to moan piteously.

Sam's feet were loosely tied. She kicked, loosening her bonds even more and allowing her to wriggle closer to her sister. She patted Susan's leg with her foot, and Susan's moans ceased.

Sam kicked again. This time, her foot hit something heavy—the tire iron. She kept kicking until she managed to force the iron against the side of the trunk with a clang. The car stopped.

She heard the trunk open, felt a breeze, then her gag was pulled away. "Whassa matter, kid?" a voice growled.

"Bathroom," she croaked. "I . . . I gotta go."

The man cursed and yanked off the blindfold. Beside her, Susan lay in a limp, silent heap. "She has to go, too," Sam said.

"One at a time."

"Please," Sam begged. "I want her to come with me. I'm scared."

"I told you, kid. One at a time. Come on."

Her captor hauled her roughly from the car and set her on her feet. He leaned close. Even through the ski mask, his smoker's breath made Sam want to gag. "See those bushes there? I'm gonna untie your legs and let you walk over there, but I'll be right behind you." He held up his hand and something glittered in the moonlight. A knife. At least, Sam thought, he didn't have a gun.

She was shaking so badly she could hardly move, but the man gave her a shove and she began walking. She glanced around. They were at the side of a highway. They must have traveled far from town because she could see no lights. No traffic, either. She swallowed, wondering if she'd be in more danger alone on the road. No, she couldn't think of that. She had to get away, and she had only one chance.

They reached the bushes. She hesitated.

"Okay, kid," the man ordered. "Get it over with. We got a long way to go."

"I . . . I can't. Not with you watching," she whined.

"Then you're outa luck."

"C-couldn't you just turn around?"

The man cursed. "Damn prissy kid." But he turned halfway.

Sam ran.

With a snarl, he followed. He caught up to her within seconds, grabbed her by the hair and jerked her around. "You stupid kid. Now I'm gonna have to hurt you." He raised his arm and brought it toward her, his knife flashing.

With every ounce of her strength, Sam kicked at him. He stumbled back, but not before the knife blade slashed her hand. She barely felt the pain. She turned and ran.

She didn't have time to wonder why he let her go. Now she could only think of getting away. Half an hour later, she reached an all-night service station. The owner called the highway patrol, and they took her home. Only later did she learn her captor had twisted his ankle when he fell.

Even though her ordeal was far shorter than Susan's, months passed before she could be alone in the dark. Fear of enclosed places lasted longer. When she was in her teens, she resolved to overcome it. She'd always enjoyed taking snapshots, so she decided to learn how to process and develop them. The first time she walked into a darkroom and the door closed behind her, she nearly fainted. The walls threatened to close in on her, but she didn't give in to her fear. Soon, the thrill of seeing her photographs come to life became stronger than her terror. The claustrophobia disappeared. She'd always thought of her photography as a symbol of the way she'd conquered her fear.

Now it returned, full force. Sweat pouring down her back, she gasped for air. The room began to spin and she sank to the floor. She felt as if someone had pressed a pillow over her face to smother her. She tried to take a deep breath, but there was no oxygen. She pressed her fists to her eyelids. "Calm down," she ordered herself. "Think of something."

She shut her eyes and pretended she wasn't in a closet but in a darkroom. Developing pictures of someone . . .

Wade.

He would come for her. Somehow he'd find her, even if he had to blow his cover sky-high by questioning Helen to find out where she'd been tonight. He might be angry that Sam had gone off without him, but as soon as he realized she was missing, he'd move heaven and earth to get her back.

Wade. As if her imaginary photograph were emerging, his face swam into view. She concentrated . . . on the dazzling blue of his eyes, his teasing smile, his lazy drawl, but most of all, on the strength and protectiveness he projected. Her heartbeat slowed, her pulse steadied. As long as she kept his image before her, she'd be all right.

WADE RUBBED A HAND over his eyes. How long since he'd had a good night's sleep? And he wouldn't be getting one tonight. The clock on the dashboard showed nearly two as he slid wearily behind the wheel and turned on the ignition. For a brief moment, he considered driving straight home and falling into bed, but he couldn't. He had to check on Sam. Had to give her a piece of his mind, too. He yawned and headed for the freeway. *She* was probably home and fast asleep by now.

He'd spent an hour questioning the creep that Carole's bodyguard apprehended and had learned that Don Juanito—the bastard—had hired himself a hit man. Fortunately, an inexperienced one who came clean the minute the words *cops* and *prison* were mentioned. Wade had happily turned him over to the two officers who'd come to the house. When they'd finally gone, he'd spent another hour with Carole, trying to calm her, assuring her it was unlikely her husband had hired *two* hit men, and in any case, the bodyguard would protect her. Finally, he'd suggested she move into a hotel under a false name, with the guard stationed outside her door. He'd followed her to the Omni, checked her in and left her with more assurances that nothing else would happen.

Now to see about Sam.

He turned into her driveway at two-thirty and drove slowly to the guest house. It was pitch-dark. Sam's Volvo wasn't in front.

He didn't bother to shut the door as he jumped out of his car and ran to the entrance. He knocked. No one answered. He pounded. Nothing. The house was as silent as a tomb.

The flash of fear he'd felt before came back and multiplied until it stormed through him, turning his blood to ice.

He tore back to the car and burned rubber speeding out of the Brewsters' driveway. Visions of Peter played in his mind like an old horror movie. Peter walking confidently into the building where he was to meet his contact, his body arching as the bullet hit, then falling, falling, slamming to the floor. And the red ribbon of blood. Had Wade subconsciously allowed his partner to go in first to save his own life? He'd never been able to answer that question, and he'd never gotten over the guilt.

And now—oh, God, no! Not Sam. He should never have taken this case, never have agreed to work with an amateur. But, selfish bastard that he was, he'd done it for his book. Had he sacrificed Sam for a few weeks on the bestseller list?

He took the road at breakneck speed. If his pal from earlier in the evening was still giving out tickets, the guy would have a high-speed chase on his hands because Wade wasn't stopping for anything this time.

He made it to Garrett Franklin's building in record time, gave the guard at the parking garage a song and dance and drove through the entire three floors of parking spaces, searching for Sam's car. She wasn't there.

He hit the freeway and headed for Helen's. The house was dark; the porch light, which had been on earlier, was turned off. Helen's car sat in the driveway, but he saw no sign of Sam.

He called her house, her car, even her office, and got no answer. He wanted to scream out his rage and frustration, beat his hands against the windshield. He couldn't. He settled for muttering a few prayers. They couldn't hurt.

He made a U-turn and sped back toward Sam's. If she wasn't home by now, he'd call the police. Hell, he'd call the Texas Rangers, the FBI. He swore viciously as he took the freeway ramp. He'd find her. He had to, or he'd go mad.

HALF DOZING, Sam slumped in the corner of the closet. Images swam in and out of her mind—an icy stream, a soft bed, a banquet table piled high with every delicacy she could imagine. She'd taken herself on imaginary trips to places she'd always wanted to visit—Morocco, Mount Kilimanjaro—had held make-believe conversations with Joan of Arc and Anne Boleyn and had solved a dozen cases with the ease of Sherlock Holmes. Whenever her fantasies failed to calm her, she returned to the image of Wade. Always Wade, with his hand on her shoulder, his deep voice soothing, promising that everything would soon be all right.

Now, even that wasn't enough, so she imagined more. She pictured him making love to her, felt his hands on her body, his lips on hers. Then, lost in her fantasies, she forgot for a while where she was.

Her head fell forward and startled her awake. She blinked. The luminous dial of her watch read two-fifteen. She shifted and the movement brought on a charley horse in her right calf. She worked at the painfully knotted muscle, wishing she had room to walk.

A sudden noise diverted her attention from the cramp. Had she imagined the sound? No, she heard it again—the rattling of some kind of cart. And voices! "...and I'll start back here."

The cleaning service. Thank God!

She pulled herself to her feet. For an instant, she felt faint, but she brushed aside the weakness and pounded on the door. "Help! Let me out."

"What was that?" a voice asked.

"Here. In the closet. I'm locked in." She banged the door again. "Open up."

Footsteps, the click of the latch. Then light and air.

Sam lurched forward, almost stumbling into the arms of a startled cleaning lady. The woman screamed.

"Don't be frightened." Sam tried to sound reassuring, though she couldn't blame the woman. It wasn't often an intruder stepped out of a closet and practically fell at your feet.

"Who ... who are you?" The wide-eyed woman backed away.

A man hurried up. "What's wrong?"

Sam spread her arms to show she was unarmed, then manufactured a story. "I was here for the rehearsal." They stared at her dubiously, and she improvised. "I got a spot on my dress. I went to the closet to get something to clean it, and I must have pulled the door shut behind me." The two continued to stare at her silently, and she took a step toward the exit. "Thanks for letting me out." Another step. "I'll be on my way."

They said nothing. Forcing herself to walk at a normal pace, Sam headed down the hall. She opened the door and took a long breath of wonderfully cool night air. She felt like falling to her knees and thanking her lucky stars that she was free from her prison and that the cleaning people hadn't called the police, or worse, the building owner. What would Garrett Franklin have said if he'd learned she'd been there?

She darted around the corner and cut across the parking lot to her car. She sank into the seat and sat for a moment, taking deep breaths. Then she yawned. She thought of calling Wade, but he was probably fast asleep. In the morning, she'd tell him what she'd learned. All she wanted right now was a tall glass of ice water, a shower and a few hours of sleep on a soft mattress. And she never wanted to smell bleach again.

IN HER DREAM, Sam lay on a deserted beach beneath a cloudless sky. The sun warmed her, the rhythm of the waves soothed her. On her portable stereo, music played. A flute, a piano, a drum.

A drum? That didn't belong with this kind of music. But the drumbeat continued, louder and louder...

She jerked awake. Not a drum. Someone was beating on her door at—she squinted at her watch—four in the morning. Who?

A weapon. She needed a weapon. She kept Mace in her purse. Where had she tossed it when she'd come in? Damn, she couldn't remember.

Her eyes swept the room. A heavy vase stood on the chest of drawers. She tiptoed over and grabbed it, then slipped into the living room.

She edged toward the door. The pounding continued. In another minute, the visitor would break it down. How had someone gotten past the guard at her grandfather's gate? She'd have a talk with the security service tomorrow.

She peered out the peephole. A fist swung by and she heard it crash against the door. Then she saw the arm that went with the fist and followed it up past a broad shoulder to the owner's face.

Wade!

She set the vase down and opened the door. "What are you doing here in the middle of the night?"

He didn't give her a chance to answer, just marched inside. He kicked the door shut behind him, strode past her, then swung around to face her. "Where in holy hell have you been?" He was angry. Dangerously angry. His lips tightened in a scowl, his eyes were the blue of a stormy sea and his fists were clenched.

Sam refused to cower. She stuck her hands on her hips and her chin in the air. Haughtiness wasn't easy to achieve when you were clad in a rumpled T-shirt and your feet were bare, but she was determined to try. "You know where I've been."

"Yes, Your Majesty," he snarled. "I know. You've been out on a damn fool's errand."

"I was working on the case."

"Alone, damn it." He grabbed her shoulders and shook her. "I told you not to go without me."

His fingers tightened. Tight enough to bruise, but Sam stood her ground, her eyes on his. "You didn't show."

"I was late. I called, and what did I get?" He shook her again. "Your machine at home and another out-of-the-service-area recording in your car. You didn't change the battery, did you?"

Sam's cheeks flushed. "No."

"Do you know how many times I tried to reach you?" he shouted. "Why didn't you call me? Do you have any idea how worried I've been?"

She hadn't given that a thought. Puzzled, she stared at him. His face was a mask of fury and frustration. "Why?"

He stared at her as if she'd lost her mind. "Why?" He let out a ragged breath. "Because I want you safe. I want you in one piece." His hands gentled on her shoulders. "Damn it, Sam," he muttered, "I just want you."

Their gazes locked. She must have made some sound of assent because in less than a heartbeat, she was in his arms, his mouth on hers, his hands in her hair.

All those fantasies she'd had of him when she was locked in the closet had been pale imitations of the real thing. They'd only been pictures. Now she had his scent, masculine and potent. Now she had the sound of his moan in her ears, the taste of his tongue in her mouth, the feel of his arms pulling her closer.

This was no planned seduction. There was no finesse, only raw need. His mouth open on hers, he kissed her as if he were starving. His hands racing over her body, he touched her as if he were blind, as if he could read her innermost secrets through her skin.

He overwhelmed her. She'd always kept her head, always been in control with a man. Now she was reduced to a mass of quivering nerve endings, riotous emotions. Yet she felt powerful, too. She was primal woman—Eve or Lilith—mating with her man.

He pushed up her T-shirt and cupped a breast in his palm. His fingers splayed over it, pressing against the tight bud of her nipple. Sam gasped as another shock of primitive desire jolted through her. He yanked the shirt over her head, she tore at his, scattering buttons in her haste. The sight, the feel of his naked chest aroused her more. She closed her lips over his nipple, heard him groan.

His teeth scraped her shoulder, his hands roamed her thighs, cupped her buttocks. "I want you. Now," he rasped.

"Wait."

"I've already waited too long." He unzipped his jeans.

Sam tugged at his arm. "The bedroom . . ."

"Too . . . far. Here." He grabbed the condom from his pocket just before he kicked the jeans away and pulled her with him to the floor.

Hands shaking, he sheathed himself.

Panting, she lay on top of him. She felt him hard and hot against her thighs. And she was ready for him as she'd been for no other man. With a cry—desire? triumph?—she reached for him and took him.

Like a glowing torch, he spread fire through her. His arms locked her to him, his eyes glittered like blue-black coals as his heat seared her deep inside. They rocked together, fast, faster, fanning the flames. And then she shattered, hurtling over the edge. An instant later, Wade followed.

They lay still, too spent to move or separate. Sam's head rested on his shoulder. Only her tongue moved, slipping out to lick his salty, sweat-soaked skin.

"Mmm," he murmured.

"Wow!" Sam sighed languidly. "This is the first time I've made love in a doorway."

"This is the first time I've made love with someone named Sam."

She raised her head and met his eyes. The teasing glint was back and he wore a satisfied smile.

"Yep, first time," he continued, "but it won't be the last." He urged her down for a kiss. "Where's your bedroom, darlin', and I'll show you."

Sam slipped out of his arms and they both stood and began gathering their scattered clothing.

"Bedroom's right this w—" Sam stopped midsentence as a loud thumping on the door interrupted.

"Ms. Brewster, Ms. Brewster, it's me, Nate. Are you all right?"

"It's the security guard," Sam whispered. "Yes, Nate," she called. "I'm just fine."

"I saw a car in the driveway, and I thought I'd better check on you."

"Thanks, but everything's okay. The car belongs to a ... business associate." The business associate came up behind her, licked her nape and reached around to cup her breasts.

"Okay then. Night, Ms. Brewster."

Sam didn't answer. She'd turned from the door and her mouth was occupied, fastened on Wade's. "The bedroom," she reminded him after a minute.

He dropped his clothes in front of the door, swung her up in his arms and carried her to bed where, for the second time in his life, he made love with someone named Sam.

WHEN WADE AWAKENED several hours later, Sam was still sleeping. He lay still for a moment, enjoying the feel of her body pressed against him, drinking in her scent. Then, moving carefully so he wouldn't wake her, he propped himself up on an elbow and feasted his eyes on her.

She was so beautiful, one of those rare women whose every feature was perfect. And her hair. Until she'd opened the door a while ago, he'd never seen it down. Now it curled across the pillow, so golden he wondered if Samantha had trapped the sun. She'd caught its heat, too. The first time he'd seen her, he'd sensed fire beneath the ice, but he hadn't known it was a raging inferno.

With his eyes, he traced the curve of her breast. She was more than heat; she was passion. And generosity. Even as she took him, she'd given—wild excitement, stunning pleasure. And afterward, when they'd lain spent in each other's arms, she'd given him tenderness. He'd felt contentment spread through him like a soft blanket, like glowing embers after the flames had died. He felt as if he'd found a part of himself that had been missing. As if he'd fallen—

No! That was his writer's imagination working. A spasm of fear clutched his stomach. He sat up quickly, swung his feet off the bed and went into the living room to retrieve his clothes.

When he fastened his jeans, his hands shook. He couldn't fall in love with Samantha. If he did, he'd be a mass of raging nerves every time she did anything remotely dangerous. He'd never be able to work with her. That was hard enough already. No, he'd keep things light between them. Sex, not love. Right.

He gathered up his shirt and Sam's and put them in the bedroom, then padded barefoot into the kitchen. After putting the coffee on, he got bacon and eggs from the fridge and started the bacon. He was rummaging in the cabinet, looking for another pan for the eggs, when he heard Sam's voice behind him. "I thought you'd gone."

"No, I decided to make—" He turned and swallowed. She'd put on his shirt but had left it unbuttoned. His gaze traveled from her slender throat downward, past a tantalizing glimpse of creamy breasts, the dip of her navel, a circle of golden curls and the mystery below them. Instantly, he hardened. "—breakfast," he croaked.

She took a step toward him. He backed up. His rear collided with the counter. "What's wrong?" Sam asked.

Wrong? What was wrong was that he was so aroused from the sight of her that he was in danger of becoming the only man in history to climax just by looking at the object of his desire. He needed a cold shower. He needed to keep things light. He needed Samantha.

The frying pan in his hand clattered to the floor. He covered the distance between himself and Sam in an instant and pulled her into his arms. "What's wrong," he muttered against her mouth, "is that I haven't kissed you in an hour."

Her tongue teased his and desire overwhelmed him. He undid his jeans, kicked them off and lifted her. Her legs wrapped around him as he carried her to the nearest chair.

She was hot and wet and open for him. And, God, he was ready. He couldn't have waited another minute. He thrust inside her, shut his eyes and let the fire consume him.

Heat. Even afterward, he could feel it, almost smell it.

"Wade." Sam's voice was urgent.

"Hmm?" With an effort, he opened his eyes.

"The bacon's burning."

"Oh, hell." He set her on her feet and ran for the stove. A hissing panful of charred meat met his eyes. He grabbed the pan and dumped it in the sink. So much for bacon. "How about toast?" he called over his shoulder.

"Hmm?" She looked shell-shocked.

"Toast?"

"I have bread in the pantry," Sam said and went to get it, wobbling a bit as she walked—from all that strenuous lovemaking, Wade thought, pleased.

In a few minutes, they were seated across from each other. Wade buttered his toast, then made the mistake of glancing at Sam again. His gaze shot straight to her breasts. Damn, not again. He'd promised himself to keep things light. "Button that shirt, would you," he said, "or this may be a real short breakfast."

Sam chuckled and complied.

Even with no skin showing, he wanted her, but with the shirt buttoned, he found it marginally easier to abstain and focus on something else. "What happened last night?"

Sam's eyes sparkled. "I found out what Helen's notes were about."

Wade listened as she explained. "Good work," he said after she finished.

Sam grinned, then her smile disappeared. "But Garrett wants something from Helen." She repeated their conversation. "And that's all I heard before they left."

"So Helen's not off our list yet," Wade mused aloud. "She might have stolen the recipe, but Garrett wants something more from her and I doubt it's pointers for making pie crust. We'll keep watching her. Garrett, too." Then a thought crossed his mind. Play rehearsals didn't last half the night; the conversation Sam reported had been a short one . . . He glanced sharply at her. "What took you so long to get home?"

Sam's cheeks colored. "I wasn't that late."

"Hell, darlin', the first time I checked here, it was two-thirty. That ain't early."

She stared at her toast as if it were suddenly of major importance. "I was detained."

"Yeah? Where?" When she didn't answer, he scowled at her. "Where, Sam?"

"In a broom closet."

"What!"

"A closet," she repeated. "I, uh, got locked in."

He shot out of his chair and marched around the table. "Damn it," he roared, "you could have suffocated."

"Calm down, Wade. Don't be ridiculous."

But he was just warming up. "You could have—" As his voice rose and his muscles clenched, the thought occurred to him that they were back to normal, yelling at each other like banshees. If he could keep his mind on Sam's incompetence, maybe he could block out the emotions that threatened him. Maybe he could keep his head, and his heart, intact.

TWO HOURS LATER, Wade opened the door to his office. The odor of nail-polish remover hit his nostrils as he walked in.

Carla looked up from the manicure she was concentrating on and waved. Or maybe she was drying her nails. "Look who's late this morning," she said.

Wade shrugged and glanced at her, then did a double take. Each talonlike nail was painted half fuchsia, half orange. She looked like a zebra getting ready for the circus. "What's with the nails?" he asked. "Isn't it too early for Halloween?"

Carla gave him a disdainful look. "Just trying a new style." She blew on the fingers of her left hand. The phone rang and she picked it up with her right. "Phillips Investi— No, Kim, you may not. No and that's my final word." She slammed the phone down and began rifling through a paperback entitled *I Say No and Mean It: Affirmations for Parents of Adolescents.* "Can you believe she called me from school? She's been pestering me to let her get a Mohawk haircut. A girl, for God's sake. Where does she get these weird ideas?"

"Maybe she has a role model," Wade suggested, gazing pointedly at Carla's nails.

She scowled at him again, then fished out the message book. "Harold called."

Great day, Wade thought as he picked up the phone and punched in his agent's number. "Harold, what's goin' on?"

"What's going on with you?" Harold growled. "Francine tells me you've asked for another extension. What is it with you—you got a death wish?"

"I'm rewriting one of the characters."

"Why? You're not late enough as it is? Your publisher is going to tear up your contract, and you know what? I'll help."

"Take it easy, Harold. The way I've changed her, the character will be more appealing." He wasn't sure he believed that, but for Sam's sake, he needed to make the change. He tuned out Harold's curses and waited for his agent to take a breath. As soon as Wade could get a word in, he said, "Gotta get back to work."

"See that you do."

Wade hung up, turned on his computer and inserted the disk he'd brought from home.

Nick lay in Al's bed, her body wrapped around his. When he started to get up, she caught his arm. "Stay the night."

Nick shook his head. He never stayed all night with a woman, no matter how great the sex. He turned away.

She stroked his back. "I need you, Nick."

"Don't," he said. "Don't get any ideas. What's between us—it's a short-term thing."

Wade read over what he'd written. The scene left him dissatisfied, without his usual feeling of kinship with Nick.

The fault wasn't with Nick. It was Wade who'd behaved out of character. His fictional counterpart was his usual self.

Nick Petrelli would never stay long enough to burn the bacon.

7

CARRYING THE PLASTIC cartons of chili from Arnold Stewart's restaurant, Sam strolled leisurely across the lawn toward her grandparents' house. A soft breeze whispered against her cheeks and brought the scent of newly mown grass. She took a deep breath, then glanced upward. Through the moss-laden trees, she glimpsed a golden half-moon.

She smiled. Life was good. She'd come a giant step closer to her goal of becoming a private detective, and she'd uncovered valuable information about one of the prime suspects in the theft. And done so single-handedly, at that.

And, of course, there was Wade. The thought of him and the magic they'd made together sent a current racing through her. She'd never felt so wild, so greedy for a man, as she'd felt the other night and this morning . . . and every time she'd thought about him during the day. No one she knew—herself included—could have imagined the self-contained Samantha Brewster writhing on the entry-hall floor and relishing every minute of it. Sam laughed softly. But of course, no one would ever know . . .

Unless Wade put it in his book.

The nagging thought of his other life had plagued her throughout the day. Surely he wouldn't write about something so personal. Or would he? He based Nick Petrelli on real life. Did that mean investigative work only or did he include love affairs? Wade admitted he liked women—his tone had indicated "women" with a capital *W*. Sam kicked at a rock as she crossed the driveway. She'd die of embarrassment if she showed up in Wade's next book, even if she and Wade were the only people who recognized her. She'd just have to convince him to let her read his manuscript. Maybe after their meeting with her grandfather...

Nearer the main house, she picked up speed. Clint had said eight o'clock and he didn't like to be kept waiting.

She rang the bell and Harrison opened the door. "Your grandfather is in the living room, Ms. Brewster."

"Thank you. Would you put these cartons in the refrigerator for me?" She handed them to the butler and hurried into the large, elaborately furnished living room. "Hi, Granddad."

Clint rose from the sofa and enveloped her in a hug. "How are you, princess?" he said.

Funny, Sam thought, Wade had told her she reminded him of a princess, too. "Fine. How was England?"

"Good but tiring. Your grandmother went to bed right after dinner." He patted a place on the couch. "Tell me what progress you've made on the case." Before she could answer, he added, "You getting along all right with Phillips?"

"Uh-huh." Sam gave her grandfather an innocent smile.

"Good. I want you two to have a compatible relationship."

"We *are* compat— That is, we do have a good working relationship." The doorbell saved her from having to say anything more.

Sam sprang up, but Clint shook his head. "Sit. Harrison will get it."

Sam heard Wade's voice at the front door and listened to his booted feet coming down the hall. He entered the living room and her pulse jumped to double time as he came toward them with that confident, macho swagger. He was wearing a Western shirt and a pair of faded jeans that Sam found all the sexier because she knew what was underneath . . . and what it could do to her. Their eyes met, held, then just before he extended his hand to Clint, he turned away from her grandfather and winked at her. Nick Petrelli himself couldn't have made a better entrance.

Wade and her grandfather exchanged pleasantries, then Clint motioned Wade to a chair. As soon as Wade was settled, Clint looked from him to Sam. "Well, any news?"

Wade summarized the events of the past two weeks. Sam was pleased that he gave her copious credit for solving the riddle of Helen's notes *and* that he omitted any mention of her incarceration in the closet. "Sam, did you bring the chili samples from Stewart's restaurant?" he asked.

She nodded.

"Good. We'd like you to give them a try," he told Clint.

They went into the kitchen and Sam got the cartons from the refrigerator. She'd marked each with the name that appeared on the menu. She popped them in the microwave while Clint got a spoon out of the drawer. "Want a beer, Phillips?" he asked.

Wade declined, as Sam expected. She'd already poured his usual ginger ale. Her arm brushed his as she leaned forward to set the glass in front of him, and her grandfather glanced at her sharply. Sam turned away.

When the oven timer went off, she brought Clint the first carton. "This one's called Bronc Buster." She sat at the table and watched as Clint tasted.

He took a bite, rolled the chili around on his tongue like a wine taster, held it in his mouth for a moment, then swallowed. "Bah!" He made a face. "That's a lame excuse for chili. May be good for a tenderfoot or a little kid, but no real chili lover would waste his time on it."

"I, um, guess that's not ours," Wade said, grinning at Sam.

"You better believe it, son. I'd have been dead broke if I'd marketed some fool concoction like this. Look at that." He gestured disdainfully at the pinkish brown mass in the carton. "Even the color's tame."

Sam chuckled. "Ready for the second?" She read the name on the carton. "Red Devil."

Clint muttered something under his breath. "Bring it on."

She placed the next carton in front of him and he tasted. Then, spoon in hand, he stared at the chili as if he thought it might leap off the plate and bite him back.

"Well?" Sam asked.

"This isn't chili."

"But the menu said—"

"The menu's wrong."

Sam sniffed. "It smells like chili."

"No," her grandfather roared, "this isn't chili. Arnold Stewart should be shot. Damn dish is full of beans. No self-respecting cook dirties up his chili with *beans*."

"Blasphemy," Wade agreed, grinning. "Adding beans to chili is as bad as puttin' a sidesaddle on a cow pony."

"Uh-oh," Sam said. "I guess we didn't notice."

"How about recipe number three—Flamethrower?" Wade suggested.

Again Clint went through the tasting ritual. This time he merely wrinkled his nose. "Not bad, but it has too much cinnamon for my taste."

"So none of them are yours," Wade said.

"Not a one."

"That eliminates Arnold Stewart's restaurant and drops him lower on the list. Helen Kay and Garrett Franklin are still near the top."

"What about finding the guys who entered the cook-off?" Clint asked.

"No luck so far, but that's our next step," Wade said. "We head for the nearest competition and see if the Hot Hombres turn up again. Sam, call that lady from the chili society—the Green Pepper."

"The *Great* Pepper." She made the call and announced, "The next cook-off's in Flatonia on Saturday."

"We'll head out there," Wade said. "Meanwhile, we'll keep checking the possibility of an inside job." He stood. "If you don't have any more questions, Mr. Brewster, I'll be on my way." His eyes slid to Sam's. Their message was clear: *Come with me.*

She half rose from her chair, but Clint put his hand on her arm. "Stay a while. I'll see Phillips out, then we'll talk in the living room."

Sam sent Wade her own silent message: *I wish I could.* But her grandfather was also her boss at the moment. She supposed he wanted to talk about the dishes she was photographing for the company cookbook. She went into the living room and made herself comfortable on the couch.

Clint returned and sat across from her. "What's going on between you and Phillips?"

Startled, Sam stared. "Wh-what gave you the idea that anything is?"

Her grandfather leaned back and crossed one foot over the other knee. "I wasn't born yesterday, young lady. Enough sparks were flying this evening to set the house afire."

Caught. She'd never been able to sneak anything past her grandfather. "We, ah, like each other."

"In plain English, you're seeing him after business hours," Clint said.

"Yes, well—"

He caught her hand in his large one. "Don't get in too deep, honey. Phillips isn't some wet-behind-the-ears corporate pup like that last guy you got involved with. From what I hear, he's been around the block a few times. He could hurt you."

A shiver skimmed along her spine. "I know," she said, looking down at her other hand, which she'd clenched in her lap, "but I know where I stand with him."

"Where's that?"

She cleared her throat, trying to rid it of a sudden lump. "Neither of us is interested in a commitment. I want to learn everything I can from him about detective work. And he wants..."

"He wants?" her grandfather prodded.

"He wants to solve this case."

"And after the case is over?"

"We'll shake hands and each go our own way," Sam assured him, though she realized she didn't care for the sound of that.

Clint tipped her chin up and scrutinized her with shrewd blue eyes. "I hope so." He said nothing more, just gave her hand a squeeze and murmured, "Run on home now."

She bent to kiss his forehead, then let herself out the front door. The sky had darkened while she'd been inside, and the moon had risen higher. Stars blanketed the heavens, and crickets sang softly. Sam's feet crunched on the gravel driveway.

Her grandfather saw too much. Knew too much. He was right. Wade wasn't like Keith. He was a man, from his tousled hair to the tips of his boots, and he could break her heart.

Well, she wouldn't let him. She'd come away from this with her emotions intact, some good memories and a lot of knowledge about investigative work.

On the other hand, maybe their association didn't have to end with the case, she thought as her natural optimism kicked in. *Phillips and Brewster, Private Investigators*. That had a nice ring to it. If she played her cards right, maybe Wade would make her an offer. She wouldn't mind being a junior partner... for a while.

As she neared the guest house, she saw a movement in the shadows near a spreading oak tree. She paused for a moment and peered into the darkness. Certain she hadn't imagined it, she picked up a stick and inched forward.

The shadow detached itself from the tree. "You're not going to bean me with that, are you?" asked a familiar voice.

A wave of relief, then one of pleasure washed over her. "I ought to," she said, brandishing her weapon. "You scared me."

Wade took the stick from her hand and tossed it to the ground. "Come inside, and I'll kiss you and make it better."

"Kiss me now," Sam invited. She put her arms around his neck, stood on tiptoe and tilted her head.

She didn't have to ask twice. He pulled her close and kissed her with an intensity that set her mind spinning.

She felt him snap the band that held her ponytail, and her hair cascaded around her shoulders. Wade combed his fingers through it, turned his head and brought a thick strand to his lips. "Rapunzel," he murmured.

Sam laughed. "My handsome prince."

"You're beautiful."

She had barely enough breath to whisper. "When you say it like that, you make me weak."

"I want to. I want to make you tremble."

"You do," she said on a sigh.

He let go of her hair and tightened his arms around her. His eyes gleamed wickedly. "Ever made love in the backyard?"

"No, and I don't think I want to start." Sam laughed. "The security guard doesn't need a show."

Wade nipped at her lips. "He'd be royally entertained."

"Not by me, thanks." She tugged at him, and he began backing her toward the patio, kissing her with every step—her forehead, her cheeks, her chin. Giddy from the sensations evoked by his lips, Sam nearly tripped, but then she felt the French door at her back. "This is as far as we go," she murmured.

"We can go a lot farther." He unbuttoned her shirt, unfastened the front clasp of her bra and covered one breast with his palm. Sam moaned as he massaged her sensitized flesh, arousing her even more. He pressed against her, fitting his body intimately against hers, rubbing himself against her, kneading her breasts, planting hot, wet kisses in the hollow at her throat.

Sam tugged at him. "Let's go in," she panted.

They turned sideways, bumped against the door . . .

An earsplitting wail sounded, and every light on the grounds went on.

For an instant, Sam stood frozen, stunned. Then she clapped a hand to her mouth. "We set off the alarm. Come inside. Hurry!" She reached in the pocket of her jeans for her key. It wasn't there.

Muttering frantic curses under her breath, she rummaged through the other pockets. Where? Where had she put the damn key ring? She had to find it before it was . . .

. . . too late.

The security guard sprinted across the yard, Harrison and her grandfather—oh, Lord, her *grandfather*—at his heels. The guard's flashlight caught her, paralyzing her in its beam like a cornered rabbit. Wade stepped in front of her, but not soon enough. Her disarray had to have been clearly visible in the glare of the flashlight.

Sam's hands came up to her chest, to her *exposed* chest. Heat bubbled through her veins and suffused her cheeks. She wished she could sink into the ground and disappear.

"What's going on? Did you see anyone?" the guard shouted above the din.

"It's okay," Wade called. Still shielding Sam, he turned sideways and gestured toward the panes in the French door.

"Just a loose contact. Must have gotten dislodged." Lowering his voice, he glanced at Sam. "Go inside."

She turned her back to the approaching men and fumbled in her shirt pocket. *There was the key ring.* She snatched it out, unlocked the door and darted inside before her grandfather had a chance to speak to her. She slammed the door and sank onto the nearest chair. After a few minutes, the lights went off and the din subsided. The sound of male voices continued for several moments, then died away.

She heard a light knock, then Wade's voice. "Open the door, Samantha." When she did, he stepped inside and put his arms around her. "You okay?"

She shook her head. "I can't believe we set the darn alarm off, and even worse, that Granddad saw . . . what we were doing."

"He knows, anyway," Wade said calmly. "He watched every look between us this evening." He reached for the light switch. Sam batted his hand away, and he frowned. "Are you embarrassed about making love with me?"

His eyes were dark and serious. He'd taken her discomfort as a rejection, Sam realized. "No," she said. "I'm not embarrassed about what we're doing, just that he knows."

Wade's features relaxed, and he chuckled. "He give you a hard time earlier?" She nodded, and he pulled her close. "Poor baby."

Sam grimaced, still thinking about the alarm.

Wade's eyes glittered with amusement. "Heat might've set off that alarm. We probably burned right through the wires." He took her arm and steered her toward the bedroom. "Come on, darlin'. Let's go finish what we started."

THE NEXT EVENING, Sam had just arrived home and kicked off her shoes, when the doorbell rang. She looked out the peephole, concerned the visitor might be her grandfather.

When she saw Tonya, she relaxed. "Hi, come in," she said, opening the door.

Tonya breezed into the house. "Am I in time for dinner?"

"If you like frozen."

Tonya made a face and followed Sam into the kitchen. "If it's the best you can do, I guess I can manage." She perched on a bar stool and watched as Sam took two dinners out of the freezer and opened the microwave. "Where's Sherlock?" she asked, glancing around the kitchen.

"Who?"

"The great detective."

Sam shrugged as she set the timer. "How would I know?"

Tonya swung a bare, tanned leg back and forth. "Let me give you some advice, cuz. Never play poker."

Sam frowned. "What?"

"You'd make a lousy gambler. You can't hide what you're thinking. As soon as I said 'great detective,' your cheeks turned red and your eyes got all dreamy."

"Don't be ridiculous," Sam said haughtily. "He's just a business associate."

"Really?" Tonya leaned an elbow against the bar and gave Sam a guileless smile. "I'd have guessed he was more than that. The kind of guy that kisses you and makes bells ring, lights flash—"

"Okay." Sam stalked across the room, halted in front of her cousin and stuck her hands on her hips. "Who told you?"

Tonya giggled. "I overheard the security guard talking to the gardener while I was at the pool."

"Damn! I guess it's been blabbed all over the place."

"Yeah. Poor Sam. Caught in a compromising position."

Flushing, Sam swung around and stomped back to the counter. Now that Tonya knew, she'd never live down last night. She glanced over her shoulder at Tonya, wondering what it would take to buy her silence.

"Seriously, Sam," her cousin said, "how involved are you two?"

Sam let out a breath. "I...don't know. He's funny and sexy. And he's solid, too—the kind of man who's around when you need him."

"Sounds good."

"Yes, but I want more. I want him to respect me as a professional, and I know he doesn't. He thinks I'm playing at being a detective, that I'll lose interest."

"You'll just have to convince him otherwise."

"Mmm." Not as easy as it sounds, Sam thought. "And," she added, "he's only into short-term relationships." She brought glasses and silverware to the table and began setting them out. "Not that I'm any different," she added hastily.

"Of course." Tonya hopped down from the stool and went to the refrigerator. "What kind of sodas do you h— Yech! Ginger ale."

"Wade drinks it," Sam mumbled.

"Oh, he does?" Tonya got out a carton of milk. She poured two glasses and brought them to the table. "Know what I think?"

Sam shook her head.

"You probably don't want to know, but I'll tell you, anyway. I think you're in a lot deeper than you realize." She sipped her milk. "And maybe Sherlock is, too."

"I doubt it," Sam said, but she couldn't help wondering...and hoping.

FRIDAY EVENING Wade and Sam drove to Flatonia, stopping on the way for dinner at the Bon Ton Café in La Grange. The Bon Ton was a Central Texas landmark, specializing in no-nonsense home cooking—fried chicken, pot roast, steamed vegetables, mashed potatoes, and for dessert, flaky fruit cobblers or feather-light meringue pies. "This place could knock your cholesterol off the charts," Wade remarked.

After dinner, they stopped at the café's bakery and bought a package of kolaches, the Bon Ton's European pastries that were famous throughout Central Texas. They arrived in Flatonia well after dark and found the first motel filled. The second one was, too. And the third. "Lots of folks here for the chili cook-off," the clerk explained.

"Are there any other places around?" Sam asked.

"Well, there's the Riverview on the other side of town, but it's kind of . . ."

It was kind of seedy. In fact, very seedy, Wade noticed as they turned up the gravel driveway. It looked like the sort of place that would rent by the hour in a large city. But the sign in front said Vacancy. "Looks like we can stay here or in the car," he said.

"Here." Sam sighed, looking none too thrilled. But when Wade opened the door to number nineteen, he saw that in contrast to the motel's outside appearance, the room was remarkably clean. Of course, the furniture was old, and a test of the mattress revealed lumps, but the bed was bound to be more comfortable than the back seat of the car.

Sam tossed her overnight bag on the luggage rack, set her camera equipment on the dresser and gingerly sat on the armchair.

"Not the Waldorf," Wade said, "but it does have a TV. Cable, too, and in-room movies. Let's see . . . *The Centerfolds. Hot Times in Hollywood. Coed Slumber Party.* What's your pleasure?"

"I'll pass."

He turned to look at her, his princess in the run-down motel room. She'd already discarded her shoes and just the sight of her bare toes with their bright pink nails turned him on. He went to her and drew her to her feet. "We'll think of another way to pass the time. For instance," he added, his voice growing thick, "I haven't kissed you since we left Houston."

Sam stood on tiptoe. Her lips met his, and within minutes, they were undressed and in bed. Even the lumpy mattress and the squeaking bedsprings didn't deter them from making love. Nothing could dim the magic they had together.

Afterward, Wade propped their pillows against the headboard. He put his arm around Sam's shoulder, and she leaned back against him. "Shouldn't we plan for tomorrow?" she asked.

"Yeah. We shouldn't have too much trouble locating the Hot Hombres and getting a sample of their chili."

"Or taking their picture," Sam added. "We can ask a few questions, too."

Wade tightened his hold on her arm. "Let me do the talking."

"Why?"

"I don't want you taking chances. If those fellows get suspicious, things could get nasty."

Sam scooted out of his embrace and turned to face him. "Why do you keep saying things like that? Is it your machismo talking, or don't you trust me? Believe me, I know what I'm doing. I know what I'm capable of. I can be a damn good detective."

"How do you know?"

"The same way you knew when you started," Sam retorted, putting her hand to her heart. "I feel it *here*." She glared at him. "You think I'm dabbling in this, don't you?"

"I—"

"Well, let me tell you," she snapped, "I didn't go into this impulsively. I've always wanted to be a P.I."

He frowned and studied her thoughtfully. Tonya had said something about Sam's desire to be a detective going back a long way. "Tell me," he said.

Sam nodded. "It began when I was kidnapped."

"Kidnapped!" He felt as if she'd knocked the breath out of him. "When?"

"I was eleven. My sister Susan was eight. Our parents' names were in the Dallas papers all the time. 'Martin Brewster of Down Home Foods and his socialite wife, Camilla.' 'Fund-raiser at the fabulous Brewster mansion.' 'Martin, son of philanthropist Clint Brewster,' and on and on. Those society-column tidbits were a walking advertisement for ransom."

Wade heard the bitterness in Sam's voice and reached for her hand. It was ice-cold. He rubbed his palm over hers, trying to warm it. His thoughts flashed back to the evening at Garrett Franklin's party when she'd given the society columnist the wrong name. No wonder she hated publicity.

Sam continued, her voice low and devoid of expression. Wade suspected that if she let any emotion creep in, it would overwhelm her. "Two men in ski masks woke us and carried us out of the house. They blindfolded and gagged us, tied us up and dumped us in the trunk of their car." She stared into the distance as if she were reliving that night.

Wade could only imagine the terror clutching a small girl at the mercy of two faceless men. "Didn't anyone hear them?" he asked. "Where were your parents?"

"They were out. The sitter was downstairs. The kidnappers got in through a window in the utility room and used the back stairs." She drew a breath and went on. "After about an hour in the trunk, I managed to get loose and make enough noise to get them to stop the car. I convinced one of the men

I had to go to the bathroom, and when he untied me, I ran. Before I got away, he cut my hand."

Wade's eyes shot to the scar he'd noticed the first time they'd met. He lifted her hand and pressed his lips to the thin white mark. He felt the pain. *He* felt her fear. God, if he could get his hands on that man now, he'd murder him today for that long-ago crime.

"I walked until I got to a service station," Sam said. "The owner called the highway patrol."

Wade could hardly stand to hear any more. He pulled Sam into his arms and cradled her close. "You were brave," he whispered into her hair. *Incredibly brave*, he thought. Alone on a dark road, wondering if any car that passed could be the kidnappers returning or someone else just as bad.

"They put out an APB," Sam said, "but I couldn't describe the car so they couldn't find it. I told the police everything I knew, and they kept telling me I was a big help."

"You were."

She laughed bitterly. "Not really. All the police and we could do was wait. And all I could think about was Susan and why I didn't figure out some way to get her away from them, too."

"What else could you have done? You were only a kid."

"*I* got out. I've always felt guilty about that."

He felt her tears against his cheek. No words could erase her pain. He held her close and stroked her back.

"The next day, we got a ransom note," she said. "The police told Dad to buy time with the kidnappers while they searched for Susan."

"How long until they found her?" Wade asked.

"*They* didn't find her. After a week with no luck, Dad hired a private detective. He found Susan."

"Was she okay?"

"Yes and no. They didn't harm her, but the experience left its mark."

Wade nodded. "I understand."

"The detective found her in only two days," Sam continued. "He was wonderful."

"That's what gave you the idea of being a P.I." Her goals, her determination, even her stubbornness—everything made sense to him now.

She sat up and wiped her eyes. "You remind me of him."

Wade's heart lurched, but he tried to make light of her comment. He forced himself to smile. "I'd have found her. So would you."

"Think so?" When he nodded, she smiled and her eyes shone. He leaned forward and kissed her, very softly, very gently, then lay down and eased her into his arms. Within a few minutes, her deep, even breathing told him she'd fallen asleep.

Wade lay awake, thinking of the eleven-year-old who'd fought her way out of a kidnapper's clutches, who'd braved a deserted highway and who'd nursed a dream. A day ago, an hour ago, he'd have told her she should forget the idea of private investigating, become a lawyer or a doctor or something more suitable. Now he thought differently.

But how could he encourage her when he knew too well the dangers she'd have to face? How could he ignore his own fears, his own guilt? Sleepless, he lay in the darkness, questions plaguing him.

What did she mean when she said he reminded her of the P.I. who'd found her sister? He tried to imagine the detective through the eyes of a child. What had she seen? A hero? Wade knew he was far from that, and if Sam saw him that way, she'd be disappointed. A savior? Protector? He could be that for her, *wanted* to be, but she would come to resent him. In fact, she already did.

Tonya's words came back to haunt him. *Sam will tell you why she wants to be a P.I. when she trusts you enough.* The responsibility of living up to that newfound trust weighed heavily on his heart. For he felt certain that before long, he would be the one to hurt her.

8

WADE AND SAM ROSE early, stopped to buy coffee at a convenience store and took their breakfast to a small park across the street. They found a picnic table and, as they sipped coffee and ate the kolaches they'd brought from the Bon Ton, enjoyed the perfect October day. The sun shone from a cloudless sky, and the air held just enough nip to remind them it was fall. When they finished, they headed for the cook-off at the fairgrounds, which the convenience-store cashier had told them was on the east side of town.

Flatonia was indeed flat, part of the coastal prairie running from the Gulf of Mexico to Central Texas. "It looks like the place that time forgot," Sam remarked as they drove through the deserted downtown.

"Probably used to be a railroad stop," Wade said, pointing to the tracks that paralleled the main street. "But when trucking took over and the highway passed it by, the town died. At least it has a chili cook-off."

A few minutes later, they arrived at the fairgrounds, a flat, grassy field with vans and motor homes haphazardly parked around it. Wade parked the BMW between a van with Chilihead painted in black on the side and another with chili cook-off stickers plastered on the windows.

On the gates to the fairgrounds were banners proclaiming this event a CASI-sanctioned cook-off. Wade paid their admission and they picked up spoons and plastic cups for sampling chili. Once inside, they joined the milling crowd. Noisy conversation and laughter, family sounds—crying babies and screaming children—met their ears. Signs designating the show's sponsors—a beer company, a manufacturer of portable gas stoves, and, appropriately enough, Sam thought, the makers of an antacid—fluttered in the air. The smell of spices mingled with the odor of crushed grass.

"Let's get the lay of the land," Wade suggested. Sam nodded, pulled out her camera and began snapping pictures.

Booths belonging to the various contestants were set up on the perimeter of the grounds. The Red-Hot Mamas, two well-endowed women in denim skirts and plaid blouses, waved at them. "Y'all come on over here and try a sample of the best chili in Texas," one of the Mamas called.

"We'll be back later," Wade told her.

"Okay, handsome. We'll save you the hottest we've got."

Wade tipped an imaginary hat to her, and Sam punched his shoulder. "Come on, *handsome*. We have work to do."

"I am working," he said innocently. "Checking out the cooks."

Sam gave him an arch look. "The Hot Hombres are male," she reminded him.

They continued their survey, passing a row of stands selling beer and sodas, a sno-cone stand, booths selling all sorts of items connected with chili—scarves, earrings, posters, T-shirts. One booth offered subscriptions to *Chili World Magazine*. Clearly, chili was big business.

In the center of the grounds stood a tent with a large blue sign that said Judging and a stage where a country-western band was warming up.

They came to more chili booths—the Best Little Chili House in Texas, Los Banditos Rojos, Chiliwilli—

"There they are, the Hot Hombres!" Sam exclaimed and focused her camera on the booth. After she'd taken a few shots, she turned to Wade. "What do we do now?"

Remembering the decision he'd made during the night, he cleared his throat. "We split up." Sam stared at him in surprise. "I'll scope out the crowd for anyone we know. You go over there and see if you can charm some information out of the Hot Hombres. I'll meet you by the soft-drink stand in twenty minutes." She took a step away, and he caught her arm. "Sam, be careful."

She gave him a disgusted look. "Oh, I will. I'll try not to eat too much cotton candy."

As he watched her walk away alone, Wade had a sudden need to grab her and pull her back. But he'd made a promise to himself while she slept. He wouldn't interfere with her dream. He'd stay close enough to come running if trouble arose, but far enough away to let her try her wings, no matter how much it cost him. Tamping down the nerves that assailed him even in the nonthreatening environment of a chili cook-off, he clenched his fists and forced himself to stand still and watch her go.

SAM AMBLED TOWARD the Hot Hombres, stopping every few feet to take pictures. Not wanting to look too interested in the Hombres, she halted at several other booths and chatted with the cooks. But she didn't ask for samples of chili. Cook-offs provided only one plastic cup per visitor. She didn't want to mix recipes.

When she thought she'd spent long enough at the neighboring booth, she sauntered over to the Hombres. Both tall, wiry young men, they were wearing matching Truckin' to Terlingua T-shirts, faded jeans and boots. "Howdy, want a taste?" one of them said.

"Sure." Sam held out her cup.

The fellow dipped a ladle into the big cast-iron kettle simmering on a gas burner and filled her cup halfway.

Sam took a bite. Her eyes widened as the chili burned her mouth and throat. "Man, this is hot," she choked. "What's in it?"

"We can't tell you that, ma'am," Hombre number two said. "It's a secret recipe."

"Really? Where'd you get it?"

"From our granddaddy."

No, from my granddaddy, Sam thought, but she gave the young man a smile that invited him to continue.

"He's been makin' it around fifty years." The young man chuckled. "He used to make moonshine, too."

"I'd like to talk to him. Is he here?"

"Naw," Hombre number one replied. "He's gettin' too old to travel."

Sam nodded and took another bite. Her grandfather had said his new chili was hotter, but this recipe could scorch your digestive tract. She wished she'd bought a soda. "So I guess your grandfather used to compete at cook-offs," she said.

"Yeah."

"No."

They both spoke at once. "Well, uh, not really," the first one mumbled.

"He really didn't do cook-offs, or he really did?" Sam asked.

Obviously uncomfortable, the two men looked at each other. "Entering was sorta our idea."

His partner nodded. "Yeah, that's right. Our idea."

Sam smiled at them. "Good for you. How long do you cook this stuff, anyway?"

They glanced at each other again. "Um, a long time," number one said, and number two nodded vigorously.

"Well, I hope you win."

"This contest counts on next year's scores. We already got enough points to qualify for Terlingua," Hombre number two informed her, puffing out his chest.

"Wow, I'm impressed," she gushed. "Could you...I know this is an imposition, but this is the best chili I've tasted, and I'd like to have some extra to take home." Hating herself for it, she batted her eyelashes at them. "If you wouldn't mind."

The fellow actually blushed. "Why, sure." She handed him her cup and he filled it to the brim.

"Thank you. Now, if you two would just smile so I can get your picture." She backed up and snapped. "Thanks again," she called and waved.

Pleased with herself, Sam headed for the soft-drink stand. She had a good-size sample of chili for Clint, pictures of the Hot Hombres and a strong suspicion those two bozos were no more chili cooks than she was.

She stopped for a moment to adjust her camera bag. From out of nowhere, a blond man wearing a blue Western shirt barreled toward her. Sam gasped and jumped sideways, but he changed direction and lunged into her. She let out a cry as she fell to her knees. Chili spilled from her cup and splattered down her blouse and onto the ground. The cup dropped from her hand.

The man turned as a crowd began to gather. She thought he would extend a hand to her, ask if she was hurt. Instead, cold green eyes met hers, and very deliberately, he crushed her chili cup under his boot.

He glanced at her camera. His fist clenched. "No!" Sam shouted. If he thought he could smash it, he was wrong. She crouched over it, shielding it with her body.

The man cursed and turned away.

"Are you all right, miss?" a voice asked.

"Fine, just a little messy." Still grasping her camera, Sam pulled herself to her feet. Her palms hurt where she had scraped the ground, but she ignored the pain. She tried to keep her eyes on the man who'd hit her, but he disappeared into the crowd.

"Looked like he meant to hit you," a woman said. "Do you want to call a police officer?"

"I'm sure it was an accident," Sam said. "Really, I'm okay."

Suddenly, she caught sight of her assailant. Pushing past the onlookers, she hurried after him as he darted between two booths. Behind the booths was a rutted field with more parked vehicles scattered across it. Sam started toward the cars, then paused. The fellow wouldn't try to run her down, would he?

Uncertain whether to risk chasing him, she stood on the edge of the field, shading her eyes against the bright morning sunlight. The roar of an engine caught her attention, and she stood on tiptoe. A white Chevy pickup plowed by, spitting gravel as it passed. The blond man was at the wheel.

Sam grabbed her camera, aimed and snapped as the truck roared away. If nothing else, she'd have the license number.

She swung around and paused for a moment to examine her hands. Blood oozed from the cuts crisscrossing her palms. "Damn!" she muttered, then glanced down at her blouse. Chili stained the front. She'd have to clean up as best she could, then go back and charm another cup of chili out of the Hot Hombres.

She brushed off her jeans and headed for the sno-cone stand. She'd already noticed that the fairgrounds didn't offer amenities other than portable rest rooms, so a cup of ice would have to do for washing.

As she neared the stand, she saw Wade. *Uh-oh*, she thought, realizing she'd been gone longer than the twenty minutes they'd agreed upon. Even from ten feet away, she could sense the anger and impatience radiating from him. She braced herself for a lecture.

WADE'S PATIENCE was nearly at an end. Sam had promised to meet him in twenty minutes. Nearly an hour had passed. He'd forced himself not to track her down at the Hot Hombres' booth, but now—

Suddenly, he saw her sauntering toward him as if she had all the time in the world. Even more annoyed, he started forward. When he reached her, he growled, "What took you so l—" Then he noticed her mussed hair and the stains on her shirt. "Sam! What's wrong?"

"Nothing," she said airily. "I just had a little skirmish with a cowboy."

Fear shot through him, then rage. If someone had tried to hurt her, he'd— "What happened?" Forgetting his vow to give her the space to make her own mistakes, he grabbed her hand.

She winced. He turned her palm up and saw the blood. "You're hurt." His voice shook.

"No big deal," she said, but he must have turned pale because she laughed. "Come on, Nick Petrelli. A couple of drops of blood won't make you faint, will it? Need a soda to revive you?"

He ignored her teasing. "How did this happen?"

"I'd just left the Hot Hombres, when a man ran into me, on purpose I think. I scraped my hands when I fell."

"You fell!" He dropped her hand and took her by the shoulders, standing back to scrutinize her from top to toe. "Are you hurt anywhere else?"

"I'm fine."

"Fine," he muttered.

"Wade," she said in that extra-quiet voice that meant she was mad enough to clobber him, "that's enough. You're overreacting."

He knew he was. Still, he wanted to scoop her up in his arms and carry her away from even the slightest possibility of danger. He wanted to build a cocoon around her and keep her safe. But then he remembered her words from last night and contented himself with growling, "I told you to be careful."

Sam stepped back and raised her chin. "I was, and I'm *all right*." Her tone was cold enough to freeze Lucifer. But her eyes spat fire.

"Good," he said, forcing himself to control his emotions. "Let's get you cleaned up."

"All right, and then I have something to tell you," she said, still cool.

He took her arm and pulled her over to the sno-cone vendor. He asked for a cup of ice, then reached for her hand.

"I can do that myself," Sam said irritably.

"Forget it," he ordered and gently brushed the gravel from her palms, then cleaned them with a paper towel he'd gotten at the sno-cone stand. Looking at the bruises and scrapes on her smooth skin hurt him. He must be getting soft. "Anyplace else?" he asked gruffly.

"Just my blouse, and I'll do that myself," she said, snatching another towel from him. She scrubbed at the blouse and managed to get the chili off in some places and smear it in others. Finally, with a frustrated sigh, she gave up.

"I hope you got some good information from all this," Wade said.

"I did. These Hombres don't ring true. No way are they cooks, and they're not clear on their story, but their chili is hot enough to be Granddad's. I took their picture, and I may have gotten a shot of the man who knocked me down and one of his license plate," she said with a triumphant smile.

"How'd you do that?"

"Followed him out to the parking area when he ran off."

"You fol—" He bit his tongue. Even if Sam's actions gave him an ulcer—and they probably would—he'd have to learn to keep his mouth shut. "You made out better than I did," he said.

She smiled. "We'd better get some more chili to take back to Clint."

They headed back toward the Hombres' space. It was vacant. Their sign, their equipment and their chili were gone. Wade and Sam spent half an hour searching the premises, but could find no sign of the two men. "Where the heck did they disappear to?" Wade wondered.

"Maybe the man who hit me told them to beat it," Sam suggested. She grimaced. "There goes our chili sample."

"Maybe not," Wade said and grabbed her arm. "Come on."

He hurried across the grounds, with Sam half running to keep up. "Where are we going?" she panted.

"To the judging area," he said, pulling her along.

When they reached the judges' tent, Wade pushed open the flap and they ducked inside. Immediately, a tall, red-haired woman wearing chili-pepper earrings that dangled past her shoulders accosted them. "This area's restricted."

"I know," Wade said, "but we're investigating the theft of a chili recipe."

"Theft?" Her eyes grew wide.

"Yes, ma'am." He pulled out a card and handed it to her.

"Phillips Investigations," she muttered. "Wait here a minute." She hurried over to a tubby blond man, no taller than five foot six, and spoke to him earnestly. In a moment, she returned, accompanied by the man.

He put out his hand. "Buck Stapleton, president of CASI. What's this about a theft?"

Wade explained the situation, and Stapleton listened, frowning, then said, "We don't want any black marks on CASI's record. We're a professional organization. Our cook-offs support charities nationwide. How can I help you?"

"If you can find a sample of the Hot Hombres' chili, we'd like to take some back with us."

"Sure thing." He glanced at the judging table, where half a dozen serious-looking men and women sat tasting. "You and the little lady just wait here now, and I'll be right back."

Wade sneaked a look at Sam. He bet she was fuming inside over the "little lady," but she didn't let it show. "One more thing," he said. "Can you tell me what names the Hot Hombres gave when they registered?"

He turned to the red-haired woman. "Lettie, can you check on that?"

She nodded and hurried off.

Wade and Sam waited, and soon Stapleton returned with a plastic container. "Here you go."

A moment later, Lettie handed them a slip of paper. "Don and Dale Barkley." Wade sighed. "Same names they used in Houston."

Looking shocked, Stapleton asked, "Are you sayin' those are not their real names?"

"Afraid not," Wade told him. "The address is phony, too."

Stapleton shook his head. "I sure am sorry this happened at one of our contests. Of course, we'll disqualify the Hot Hombres from competing in Terlingua."

"No, don't do that," Wade said. "If we don't apprehend them beforehand, we may want to do it there. You know . . . catch them in the act."

Stapleton gave him a dubious stare. "We don't want any ruckus interfering with our cook-off. You know Terlingua's the international championship."

"We'll keep it quiet," Wade assured him. "No one will notice. I'll contact you ahead of time if we have to be there."

"I'd appreciate it." Stapleton shook hands with both Wade and Sam. "May Chiligula be with you."

"You, too," Wade muttered, and they left. As they headed for the car, he glanced at the chili container. "We'd better guard this with our lives. Tonight, your grandfather's having chili for dinner."

"Thank heavens the judges hadn't finished it off," Sam said. "And we have pictures, too. When they're developed, we may see someone we missed in the crowd."

"Yeah, let's head back to Houston." He slipped an arm around her waist. "Lucky we have a photographer on the team."

Sam grinned at him. "That's Brewster's first rule of private investigating, darlin'—always have a photographer with you on big cases."

Wade pulled her closer. "Especially if she looks like you."

THEY ARRIVED IN HOUSTON at one-thirty. Sam's stomach had been begging for food for the past half hour. "Let's drop the film off at a one-hour photo lab and stop for lunch," she suggested, and after depositing three rolls of film at the nearest One-Stop Photo Shop, Wade pulled up before the Mason Jar, a popular restaurant on the west side of the city.

The dining room was still crowded with lunchtime customers, but the line for tables was short. When they reached the head of the line, Wade glanced around and waved at a heavyset man lunching alone at a table for four. The fellow immediately got up and headed toward them.

"Phillips," he said, extending a beefy hand, "haven't seen you in a coon's age. Why don't you and your friend here join me?"

Wade glanced at Sam and when she nodded, he said, "Thanks." When they were seated, Wade said, "Sam, this is Hunt McClain, a P.I. friend."

Sam put out her hand, and he shook it. "And you're...?"

"Sam. Sam Spade."

McClain's mouth dropped open, and Wade chuckled. "This is Sam Brewster."

"Sam? *Your* name is Sam?"

"Samantha," Wade explained, ignoring the black look she shot him, "but she goes by Sam when she's feeling macho."

Sam dug her foot into his instep and was rewarded with a flinch. She was only sorry she didn't have on heels. They would have really hurt.

"Sam's a fledgling detective," Wade continued.

Hunt's eyes widened. "I'm surprised. I didn't think you'd take on another partner after Peter."

Sam hadn't heard anything about a former partner. She was surprised at the remark, but even more amazed by Wade's reaction. His face wore a look of such raw anguish she could feel it herself.

"Sorry, buddy. Still hurts, huh?" Hunt said.

"Yeah," Wade muttered, then picked up his menu and disappeared behind it.

Clearly contrite, Hunt shook his head. Sam could see he hadn't meant to cause Wade pain. In an effort to smooth over an uncomfortable situation and give Wade time to contain his emotions, she asked brightly, "What do you recommend for lunch?"

Though he was probably no more concerned with the cuisine at this moment than she was, Hunt gamely expounded on the restaurant's specialties. The waiter provided a further distraction. Sam ordered the baked-potato soup, and Wade mumbled, "Me, too."

When he put down his menu, he had, outwardly at least, regained his composure and they chatted amiably throughout the meal. Normally, Sam would have been fascinated by the shop talk between the two men, but right now, she was too concerned about Wade to give their conversation her full attention. Although he appeared at ease, Sam, with the intuition of a lover, knew that Hunt's comment had disturbed him more than he wanted to let on. He gripped his water glass with knuckle-whitening tension. The usual gleam in his eyes had dimmed, and his humor lacked its customary sharpness.

As soon as they left the restaurant and got into Wade's car, she said, "Still upset?"

"I'm fine."

"You weren't when we were in there."

Through his teeth, he said, "I told you, I'm okay."

Sam put her hand on his arm. He stiffened, but before he could pull away, she said, "Stop being so tough, Phillips. There's nothing wrong with showing a little human emotion when you have a good reason...and I suspect you had a damn good reason."

"Yeah, but—"

"Last night I told you about the worst trauma of my life. I know how to listen, too."

He glanced at her and sighed. Then, his voice almost robotlike, he began to speak. "Peter was my assistant. He wasn't much more than a kid, but he had the potential to be a top-notch P.I. I'd never planned to take on a partner, but I'd just made the *New York Times* bestseller list for the first time and I was snowed under, trying to meet a deadline on my second book, answering fan mail, doing phone interviews. I made Peter an offer of a junior partnership and he jumped at it. He really had the knack, but at times he could be impulsive. I knew it, but I just didn't pay close enough attention."

He paused and Sam saw a muscle twitch in his cheek. She stroked his arm, giving what comfort she could.

Finally, he began again. "A medical clinic hired us. Drugs had been disappearing and they wanted to know who was responsible. Peter nagged me to give him the case. I should have said no. He wasn't ready. I knew it in my gut, but I was so damn busy. I said yes."

Sam dreaded hearing the rest. Besides that, she ached for Wade. The muscles of his arm were coiled tight. Sweat had popped out on his forehead. "Hush," she murmured. "You don't have to tell me."

"Yes, I do. Peter started working at the clinic. Within a month, he figured out that one of the technicians had connections to a drug ring. He befriended the guy, let him know he used coke and finally set up a buy. They made arrangements to meet at an old warehouse on the north side of town.

"I had the easy job," he went on bitterly. "I was supposed to come in behind Peter, help nail the dealer. I should have been closer, covering Peter, but I didn't think it through. I'd been too busy basking in the glory of a bestseller. I left the details up to Peter."

"It was his case," Sam said.

"Yeah, and my agency."

"Yours and Peter's," she corrected.

"Not for long. I don't know whether the guy got spooked or whether he'd found out who Peter really was, but in the middle of the transfer, he pulled a gun." He swallowed. "I'd had a couple of drinks earlier. I didn't react fast enough."

"So now you don't drink at all."

"Not at work."

An awful thought burst into her mind. "Oh, God," she said. "You were right behind him."

"I don't know how I got out," Wade said. "I couldn't do anything for Peter, but I took down the bastard who shot him. I phoned the cops, then I went back to the office and called Peter's mother."

Wade turned into the photo lab's parking lot and killed the engine. Hands fastened to the steering wheel, he sat staring out the window.

Sam slid closer and put her arms around him. She understood a great deal about Wade that she hadn't before—his anxiety about her going off on her own, his anger at taking on even a temporary associate. She rubbed his back, soothing him.

At last his muscles relaxed, and he turned and kissed her cheek. "Thanks, darlin'," he murmured, then took a deep breath. "I'll go get those pictures."

Sam watched him stride into the photography shop. In the past twenty-four hours, they'd shared the most painful experience of their lives with each other. They'd gone beyond the physical and moved into the realm of emotional intimacy. She wondered how Wade would feel when he realized that. She wasn't sure how she felt, either. She hadn't planned on this closeness, this caring. She decided it was best to give it some thought.

When Wade returned with the packets of snapshots, he had apparently recovered and was his usual self.

Sam opened the first envelope. They went through the pictures slowly, looking for familiar faces in the crowd. "No one," Sam said.

The next packet was equally disappointing. They saw shots of people sampling chili, watching the cooks or just meandering through the fairgrounds. "Wait!" Sam said, picking up one snapshot. "See that man by the bandstand? I think he's the one who bumped into me."

"Do you know the guy he's talking to?" Wade asked.

Sam squinted. "No, but if we blow this up, maybe I'll recognize him. Look! Here he is again with one of the Hot Hombres. And here—" she flipped through the rest "—is his truck." She tried to read the license plate but the numbers were too small. "We'll have to blow that one up, too."

"Can they do that here?"

"No, but I can. I have a darkroom at the guest house."

Wade started the car. "A darkroom? Why didn't you develop this film?"

"They can do the rolls faster here, but I'll take care of the rest. The darkroom's makeshift. I converted a walk-in closet. It's not the best setup, but it'll give us what we need."

Wade smiled at her. "I'm impressed. And you were right, darlin'. Photographers do come in handy."

WHEN THEY REACHED the Brewster estate, Wade followed Sam into the darkroom. The converted closet was made even smaller by the addition of cabinets and a counter along one side and shelves on the opposite wall. Pans and bottles sat on the counter and the odor of chemicals—developing fluid, he supposed—permeated the air.

He followed Sam into the closet and closed the door behind them. An amber light came on. In its eerie glow, he leaned against the door and watched Sam put the first print in the enlarger. "Okay," she said. "I'll crop in on the faces and blow them up. Shouldn't take long." Wade admired the efficiency with which she worked as she adjusted the focus.

"Hand me the developing paper," she said without looking up. "It's in the cabinet next to you."

Wade bent to open the cabinet and fumbled inside. He pulled out what he supposed must be the right paper, straightened and bumped his head on the shelf on the opposite wall. "Ow."

"Be careful. It's crowded in here."

No kidding. He edged forward, the better to watch Sam work, and stood close enough to catch the scent of her perfume over the odor of chemicals. Or perhaps that was his imagination. He realized that whenever he thought of Samantha—which was often—he conjured up her distinctive scent. He leaned closer and her hair tickled his cheek.

Concentrating on her task, Sam seemed unaware of his nearness. She turned sideways, shook her head and reached for something. "Oof," Wade muttered as her elbow connected with his stomach.

"Sorry."

"'S okay." He stayed where he was, continuing to watch and enjoy her nearness. Like candlelight, the amber of the lamp touched her skin with a golden glow. In the dim light, he could make out the classic elegance of her features, the slight rise and fall of her breasts as she worked. Drinking in her scent, imagining those breasts filling his hands, he grew hard.

Sam carefully laid the paper in the developing solution and set the timer. "This should take a couple of minutes." She stepped back, smack into his chest. "Oh."

"Mmm, don't move." He looped his arms around her and bent forward to kiss the side of her neck. Her skin was smooth, deliciously warm. He nipped her neck with his teeth, then used his tongue to soothe the sting.

"Wade," she uttered breathlessly.

"Sam," he groaned, impossibly aroused by her tone, her fragrance, even the tiny panting breaths she took. "Turn around." She did. "Kiss me." Obediently, she tilted her head, parted her lips. With a groan of pleasure, he covered them with his own.

She kissed him back. He worked the band that held her ponytail loose and buried his fingers in her hair, then abandoning her hair for other, more tempting spots, slid one hand down to cup her bottom and fit her more firmly against him.

He unfastened her jeans and pushed them down, then delighted himself and her by stroking a satiny thigh.

Sam unbuttoned his shirt and kissed her way down his chest. Soft sighs of pleasure vibrated against his ribs, then a moan as he slipped his fingers inside her panties, found her center and began a rhythmic caress. She trembled, hot and slick, and wonderfully ready.

But he wanted to hear her say it. "Tell me you want me, darlin'," he whispered, his own voice far from steady.

"I want you," she moaned, shoving her jeans the rest of the way down and kicking them aside. "Hurry."

Her ardent plea nearly shattered his control. He reached for his waistband and found his own hands shaking.

Sam pushed his hands aside and took over. She undid the snap and dragged his jeans and briefs down. Her elbow bumped the lower cabinet, and she gave a pained gasp. Wade bent to help her up and dislodged something—the timer, perhaps—from the counter. He heard it hit the floor, but he was beyond caring. Heedless of the cramped room, oblivious to anything but the need to possess and be possessed, he pulled her closer. "Put your arms around my neck," he muttered. As she did, he lifted her with one strong motion. Her legs encircled him, her body pressed against his.

They were together but not together, close but not close enough and they were trapped between the counter and the shelves. "Help me," he said raspily.

"Yes." With one warm hand, she reached for him and guided him inside her.

He didn't hold back but thrust once and once again, and with a hoarse cry, emptied himself in her sweet, welcoming depths. Within seconds, her climax followed.

Afterward, they clung to each other, their hearts still pounding, their bodies slick with sweat. At last, Wade lowered her gently to her feet. She leaned against his chest and he rested his chin on her head. "You okay?" he asked.

"Mmm."

"Me, too. This is the first time I've made love in a darkroom."

He noticed that Sam didn't reply.

After a moment, he asked, "Don't you have to check the picture?"

"Oh, my gosh. I forgot all about it." She swiveled and lifted it from the developing pan, shook off drops of solution and held it up. It was jet black.

Sam choked with laughter. "It was in too long. I have to start over. This time *you* get to wait outside."

Wade didn't argue. Their frenzied lovemaking had worn him out. He didn't mind relaxing on the living-room couch with a cold ginger ale.

He'd almost dozed off when he heard Sam's excited voice.

"Come and look. I think we've hit pay dirt."

9

WADE JUMPED UP just as Sam came into the room with a handful of prints. "What've you got?" he asked.

"Here's the guy who knocked me down," she said, pointing to a seedy-looking character in a blue Western shirt standing by the bandstand. "And now we can see who he's talking to. It's one of the Hombres."

"Could be a coincidence," Wade said.

"I don't think so. Here he is again with Hombre number two. And this—" she held up the third print "—is the blowup of his license plate. SZH 248."

"Now we can track him down." Wade smiled at her. "You done good, doll."

"Yeah, I'm good to have around. But don't start calling me doll again. Not unless you want to end up on the floor."

"Only if you're with me." He took her arm and urged her over to the couch. "I'll check with the Department of Motor Vehicles tomorrow."

"What else?"

Wade leaned back and rested his feet on the coffee table. "So far, Ray Donovan's been a dead end. Bugging his house has given me his golf handicap, his barber's name and an earful of his wife's telephone conversations. Man, that lady is into gossip. I don't know beans—oops, no beans—I don't know diddly about the chili recipe, but I can tell you who's getting a divorce, who got snubbed at the latest society bash and whose hairdresser told whose secrets to whose rival." He cocked his head. "Is that the way women spend their time?"

"Not this one."

Thank God, he thought. Sam was different from most of the women he knew. Strong, feisty, determined . . . and so beautiful he could hardly believe she was real and that she was his. For a little while, at least. He reminded himself he wasn't into long-term stuff and hoped he wouldn't forget and make a fool of himself.

Forcing his mind back to the topic at hand, he said, "Since Ray seems to be off the suspect list, we need to figure out which employees have access to his login and password. I'll get your grandfather to fax me a list."

"Let's take the chili sample over for Granddad to taste."

"Okay, and the pictures, too."

They walked across the grounds to the main house and found Sam's grandparents in the solarium. The glassed-in room, furnished in wicker upholstered with bright yellows and greens, looked out on the patio, pool and gardens. A scene from *Architectural Digest*, Wade thought.

Clint greeted them and introduced Wade to his wife. Martha Brewster had the same classic features as her granddaughter. The same elegant bone structure, the same whiskey-colored eyes. She was wearing a silk blouse in copper and cream and matching copper-colored slacks. She looked as good in the outfit as a woman half her age. She might be close to seventy, but she'd still be considered a beauty. "I can see Sam comes by her good looks naturally," Wade told her. Beneath her polished exterior, he bet she had the same fiery nature.

Martha smiled, her lips curving exactly as Sam's did. "Thank you. Please sit down."

Wade and Sam sat next to each other on one of the wicker love seats. Wade let his arm rest along the back of the couch and met Clint's eyes squarely. The older man frowned. His shrewd blue eyes scrutinized Wade and Sam intensely. From the look on Clint's face, Wade could see that the older man didn't approve of the arrangement Wade and Sam had agreed upon. Probably preferred they maintain a business association or, God forbid, get married.

"So, what did you accomplish in Flatonia, Phillips?" Clint asked.

Wade deferred to Sam. She patted the plastic container on her lap. "I think we've found your chili."

"All right," Clint said. "Let's heat it up and see."

While Sam went into the kitchen, Wade handed over the snapshots. "These the same guys you saw in Houston?" he asked.

Clint held them up. "Same rotten so and so's."

"And this man? Have you ever seen him?"

Clint frowned and shook his head.

"Here you go, Granddad." Sam came in, carrying a tray with a bowl of chili. Clint needed only one taste. "That's it. That's Down Home's recipe. I don't know how they got it, but they'll pay."

"I don't think they're the ones who stole it, Granddad," Sam said. "They aren't smart enough."

"But they'll lead us to the one who did take it," Wade said. "You'll have your thief, Mr. Brewster. I guarantee it."

THE NEXT AFTERNOON, Sam sat at her desk at Down Home Foods, scrutinizing a series of photographs the color lab had just delivered. An apple pie, brimming with fruit so plump and luscious-looking she could almost taste it. A plate piled high with stew. She could almost smell the hearty aroma. Mouth watering, Sam glanced at her watch. It was after six. No wonder she was ravenous.

Wade would probably be hungry, too. They'd made plans to discuss the list of Ray's subordinates over dinner at the Great Greek. Seven, he'd said. She'd better get moving.

She stowed the pictures in her desk drawer, gathered her purse and briefcase and hurried down the hall. As she passed Helen's office, she glanced in, surprised that the light was still on. Compulsive about energy conservation, Helen never left her office without switching it off.

The door was ajar, and Helen was at her desk. Sam paused and watched as the home economist rifled through papers, scattering them over the desk and onto the floor. She grabbed one sheet, stared at it, flung it aside, then picked it up again and wadded it into a ball. Another paper got the same treatment, then she smoothed both sheets and tossed them into her briefcase. A minute later, she yanked them out again, opened her desk drawer, shoved the papers in and locked it. Odd, Sam thought as she continued toward the elevator, and very uncharacteristic.

When Sam went outside, she saw that the parking lot was almost empty. She pulled out her key and hurried to her car.

She turned on the engine and, to her dismay, heard a clanking sound. She flipped off the ignition and tried again, but the engine clanked again. *Oh, great,* she thought, turning off the engine. She'd have to call a tow truck and a cab *and* Wade to tell him she'd be late. Mr. Punctuality would not be pleased. Why, she wondered, did some gremlin interfere with her schedule whenever she had plans with Wade?

On top of everything else, it looked like rain. She might as well make her calls and wait inside the building. She got out her cellular phone, tucked her briefcase under her arm and trudged back to the building entrance.

"Do you know the number of a towing service?" she asked the security guard, who stood just outside the door.

"Yes, I can call them for you," he said. "Or do you need me to give your car a jump?"

"No, you'd better call. The engine's rattling, and I don't know—"

"Having car trouble?" said a voice behind her.

Sam turned to see Keith Nelson. "Yes," she said.

"Need a ride?"

Sam hesitated. She'd managed to avoid her ex-boyfriend lately; in fact, she hadn't seen him since the night of the Chamber of Commerce dance. He hadn't sought her out, either. She stared at him thoughtfully. By now, he was probably involved with someone else—the sultry blonde he'd kissed that night. Why not accept his offer? As long as he understood they wouldn't be lovers again, she could handle being with him. "I'd appreciate a ride," she said.

"I'll call the towing service and watch for the truck," the guard offered.

"Thanks."

Keith opened the door to a dark green Porsche. "Where to?" he asked.

"The Great Greek. I'm meeting a friend."

Keith drove out of the lot and eased into the line of cars heading toward town. He turned on the stereo and the voice of Amy Grant filled the car. Sam settled back.

The ride was uneventful. They listened to music and talked about innocuous subjects—the weather, the fall television season, a new restaurant opening near corporate headquarters. Keith made no attempt to pressure her into going out with him, and Sam was relieved.

The rain started as they drove, pelting against the roof. It looked like the kind of storm that would drench the city and slow traffic, Sam noted, more glad than ever that she hadn't had to call a taxi. She would have waited forever.

At the Great Greek, Keith pulled in under the awning. She thanked him and got out. Through the window, she saw Wade waiting for her. She hurried inside. Wade met her at the door, his face as dark as the thunderclouds that blanketed the city. He took her arm. "Why the chauffeur?" he asked.

Sam disentangled herself from his grasp. He had no right to be so possessive. They might be sleeping together, but he didn't own her. "My car had to be towed," she snapped. "Keith was nice enough to give me a ride."

Wade made no comment. Instead, he asked the hostess if their table was ready. Sam followed as the woman led them to a table directly in front of the small bandstand. When they were seated, she said coolly, "You have no reason to be jealous. I don't do musical beds."

"The thought never crossed my mind."

"Then why are you so grumpy?"

Wade sighed. "Your friend is on the list your grandfather sent me. He's one of four employees with the ability to access Donovan's login and password."

Sam stared at him. "Keith? You think he stole the recipe? That's ridiculous."

"Why? Because he's your ex-boyfriend?"

Sam paused and took a sip of water. Wade's accusation was absurd, but she saw no use in getting upset over it. She spoke quietly. "My *prior* relationship with Keith has nothing to do with this. It's ridiculous because he has no motive."

"How can you be sure?" Wade gave her a condescending look, the look an experienced P.I. gives a novice.

"I *know* him. He may be shallow and immature, but he's not dishonest."

Wade shook his head. "You know my rule. If you want to be a detective, you have to suspect everybody. Now, what do you know about the other three names on this list?"

Sam took the paper and read the names. "Bart Frazier is the assistant vice president. His wife just had twins. I'd guess he needs money more than a single man, but I don't believe—"

"Believe," he insisted. "You're too trusting, Sam."

Too trusting? No, she wasn't. For instance, she didn't trust Helen Kay not to succumb to Garrett's pressures. She wasn't sure she trusted Wade to keep her out of his current book. She didn't trust herself to withstand his charm. Darn, she was getting in over her head.

"What about the rest?" Wade said.

Sam considered. "Lana Harvey, Keith's immediate superior, is a possibility."

"Why?"

"She's a computer whiz and a talented marketer. If anyone could break into the file, copy the recipe and start a successful chili company, she could. I wonder why I didn't think of her before."

"What about Bill Drake, the liaison with the advertising agency?"

"Bill's kind of wishy-washy. Of the four, I'd say Lana was the best bet."

"I'll check them all out," Wade said.

The waiter arrived and they gave their orders, then Wade reached for her hand as he continued, "I checked the license number on the snapshot you took. The truck belongs to a guy named Jerry Snow. I got my friend at police headquarters to run him through the computer. He has a record several pages long. A couple of the charges were for assault." His hand tightened around hers.

"Ow," she gasped.

Wade seemed not to notice her discomfort. "And there you went yesterday, chasing after him on your own. Damn it, Sam, he could've—"

"But he didn't," she maintained. "Wade, you're hurting me."

He looked surprised as he glanced down at their hands. "Sorry." He loosened his hold, but leaned forward. "Sam, you have to be more careful. You could get into trouble."

"Stop it," she said. "I'm not Peter."

"No," he said, his gaze dark and intense. "You're a damn sight more . . ."

"More what?" she prodded.

"More of a pain," he said.

But Sam had the distinct feeling that he'd planned on saying something else. Just then, the waiter appeared with their meals, and she decided not to press Wade further. At times, the man irritated her beyond reason. She knew he desired her, and in bed they were equals. But in work situations, he treated her like...like a kitten. A delicate little pet that needed someone to look out for it. He forgot the strength and cunning of the cat. Darn it, Sam thought, spearing a piece of lamb with her fork, she wanted his professional respect. She'd find a way to earn it, too.

She looked up from her food. "What's our next move with Jerry Snow?"

"The next move's mine." He held up a hand to forestall Sam's objection. "I told you, Sam, he's dangerous. I'll handle him."

She let out a huff. Before she could speak, music sounded from the bandstand. A two-man combo, one playing a bouzouki and the other a guitar, had taken their places. "And now, we present our lovely belly dancer, Miss Athena Nykos."

Miss Nykos, wearing a traditional belly dancer's costume, slithered out to the sensuous beat of the music. Flowing multicolored veils revealed tantalizing glimpses of a well-filled sequin halter, and harem pants skimmed slim hips and a flat belly. Zills clicking at her fingers, she began a seductive routine that Sam knew had every man in the room, Wade included, salivating.

She glanced at him in disgust. Men were such children, so easily aroused. Look at the way his eyes bulged as the woman's navel undulated in time to the music. Look at the way he followed every sinuous movement of her arms. Look at Athena shimmying around the room, playing to the crowd. As the music intensified to a blood-stirring level, the dancer approached their table. She slithered toward Wade and draped the veil around his neck. He watched her, his eyes laughing, as she arranged the gauzy fabric over his head like a hood. She danced close, embarrassingly close, as if she was performing just for him.

Tacky, Sam decided. *Disgusting.* And the man grinned as if he'd been treated to a glimpse of heaven. As if he were a puppy wagging its tail. The number ended and Miss Nykos blew Wade a kiss. He took a bill from his pocket, folded it in half and slipped it in the waistband of her outfit. Sam sniffed. *How adolescent.*

When Miss Nykos retreated to the bandstand, Wade glanced at Sam. "Like the dancing?"

She raised an eyebrow. "It was . . . amusing."

Much to Sam's annoyance, he burst out laughing. "Want dessert?"

"No, thank you." She'd planned on having the baklava for dessert, but even though the dancer had relinquished the floor to a group of waiters doing Greek dances to the accompaniment of shattering china, Sam's appetite had disappeared.

Wade signaled for the check, and soon they left the restaurant. The rain had stopped for the moment, but fog drifted close to the ground. At the car, Sam reached for the passenger door, but Wade brushed her hand away. "Wh—" She stopped as, in a totally unexpected move, he pulled her into his arms and kissed her. She stiffened, but he paid no attention. His mouth coaxed and cajoled, nipped and nibbled.

The rat! If he thought he could placate her with kisses and caresses, he was wron...he was...he was right. Sighing, Sam leaned closer and gave herself up to his embrace.

THE NEXT MORNING, Wade drove to Spurs, a country-western café/bar on the north side of town. He'd deliberately chosen not to tell Sam that he'd learned where Jerry Snow worked. He didn't want her setting off after an ex-con on her own.

He found the place, a hole-in-the-wall located between a coin-operated laundry and an auto-parts store. The restaurant didn't look very inviting. He went inside and found a gaunt, gray-haired man seated on a stool behind the cash register. Otherwise, the place was empty. "You the owner?" Wade asked.

The man nodded. "Cade Green."

"Wade Phillips, Phillips Investigations." He held out his card. "I'd like to ask you a few questions."

Cade Green didn't look surprised. In this neighborhood, he probably got a lot of that. "Go ahead."

Wade eased onto a stool at the bar. "I'm looking for a guy named Jerry Snow. Ever hear of him?" He shoved Snow's picture across the counter.

"Yep, that's him," Cade said. "Worked for me a while. Just quit a couple weeks ago."

"What did he do?" Wade asked.

"Cook."

Bingo! Wade reached for a menu. Yep, chili was on it. "Cook," he repeated. "Was he a good one?"

"Sure was." Green ambled around the counter and sat on the stool next to Wade. "I used to do the cookin' myself, but my arthritis has gotten so bad, I can't hardly stand anymore, so I had to hire myself a replacement. Jerry turned out to be a good cook and a hard worker. He's interested in computers, too. Told me he was taking some courses at the community college. He never tried to hide the fact that he was an ex-con. I gave him a chance and he worked out pretty good. I was sorry to lose him."

"Why'd he quit?" Wade asked.

"Said he came into some money. Don't know from where, but then, I didn't want to ask too many questions." He turned shrewd gray eyes on Wade. "Don't want to ask you too many, either."

"I appreciate that. Do you happen to have Snow's home address?"

"Got it somewhere." Green shuffled back to the register, thumbed through some papers and extracted one. "Here you go."

"Thanks." Wade was about to put away the snapshots he'd brought, when a thought occurred to him. "Would you recognize either of these guys?" he asked.

Green peered at the pictures. "Why, sure. Those are the Sterling brothers—Hank and Billy Joe. They come in here pretty regular."

Hot damn! He'd hit pay dirt again. "What do you know about them?" he asked.

Green ambled over to the coffeepot. "Why don't we sit over in one of the booths? More comfortable, you know. Then I'll tell you. Want a cup of coffee?"

Wade accepted a cup of coffee that turned out to be surprisingly good, settled back in the booth and listened.

"The Sterlings are pretty good fellows," Green said. "Not the brightest, but they pay their tab, never cause any trouble. Billy Joe has a job at a gas station. Hank works on a construction crew."

"You ever see either of them with Snow?"

"Sure did. They got to be pretty good buddies while Jerry worked here."

"Know where they live?"

Green shook his head. "Not exactly. Around here someplace. I reckon you can look up their address."

"I'll do that," Wade said. He picked up the menu again. "What time's lunch?" Now that he'd found out what he'd come for, he decided to stick around, make a few notes. Nick might stop by someday.

"Whenever you want it." Green smiled, showing yellowed teeth.

"I'll try the ribs." They were the best he'd eaten in a long time.

Half an hour later, Wade emerged from Spurs, his stomach pleasantly full and his morning a success. He'd established the connection between Jerry Snow and the Hot Hombres, and Nick Petrelli had a new setting.

Now Wade had some more work to do.

He consulted his city map and located the street where Jerry Snow lived. When Wade turned onto it, he found a row of four-plex apartments that had probably been run-down for thirty years. Snow lived in the third building. Wade parked and went inside. The building smelled like a combination of bug spray, stale cigarettes and meals that had probably been cooked long ago. He grimaced and tried to hold his breath.

He found the mailboxes. Yep, Snow's name was there. Apartment C. Wade sprinted upstairs and knocked on Snow's door. He got no answer. When he knocked a second time, the door across the hall opened and a dark-haired woman peered out and surveyed him from behind thick eyeglasses. "Are you looking for Jerry?" she asked.

"Yeah, I'm his cousin. Just got in from Texarkana."

"Too bad. You should have let him know you were coming. He's out of town."

Wade smiled at her. "You wouldn't know where he's gone, would you?"

"No, all I know is he's expecting a package and he asked me to watch for it. He'll be back next week. Will you be here that long?"

Wade shook his head. "Nope. I'm sorry I missed him." He started down the stairs. He had a good idea where Snow had gone: Terlingua. He also intended to come back tomorrow night and have a look through the apartment. Tonight, however, he had plans with Sam.

When he opened the door of the pickup he drove for work, he heard the car phone. "Phillips."

"Brewster."

He grinned. Sam didn't have to identify herself. He could recognize her from her breathing alone. "What is it, dar-lin'?"

"Helen's cracking up. I heard a noise in her office just now and peeked in. Her hair's all mussed, she's pacing the floor and crying."

"Could she be rehearsing for her role in the play?"

"I don't think so," Sam answered. "This looks too real. I'm going to talk to her."

"Okay. Oh, and, darlin'—" his voice thickened "—I'll see you tonight."

"Yeah," she murmured in that sultry voice and hung up.

Wade smiled, thinking about tonight. He planned to stop by Down Home headquarters where he and Sam would try to reconstruct the computer trails of Ray Donovan's employees. He visualized making love to Sam after they'd finished. On her desk, maybe. His writer's imagination allowed him to picture the scene in graphic detail.

Then he frowned. He was becoming addicted to Sam. The idea of "short-term" seemed less attractive every day. Instead, he'd actually found himself thinking about next year, five years from now . . . the rest of his life.

He must be losing it. Sharing the good parts of life sounded appealing, but he lived with danger. Knowing Sam and her goals, he was sure she'd insist on sharing the dangerous parts, too. Uh-uh. That he couldn't handle.

SAM TAPPED on Helen's door and pushed it open without waiting for a response. The home economist stood with her back to Sam, staring out the window. "Helen."

She spun around. "Wh-what do you want?" She smoothed her hair and wiped a tearstained cheek.

"I heard you crying." Sam took a step toward her. "Can I help?"

"No, I . . ." Helen covered her face with her hands and turned away. "I'm . . . I'm . . . in a terrible mess."

This has something to do with Garrett Franklin. Sam went to Helen and put a hand on her shoulder. "Come and sit down," she said gently. Helen didn't resist and Sam led her to the couch. "Now tell me."

Helen reached in her skirt pocket and pulled out a tissue. "I almost let someone talk me into doing something awful," she said, wadding the tissue and tearing it into small pieces. "You'll have every reason to hate me."

Sam shook her head. "No, I won't."

Helen stared at her with watery eyes, then she took a breath. "I . . . I almost . . ."

Sam took Helen's hand and stilled the woman's nervous movements. "Go on."

"I almost gave away the recipe for Down Home's new chili," Helen blurted out. New tears ran down her cheeks.

This is it. She could hardly wait to call Wade. "When?"

"Today. I was going to type it out, but I—"

"Wait! You said today?"

Helen nodded. "Yes, this morning."

This morning. Then she wasn't the one who gave it to the Hombres. "Tell me what happened."

Helen got out another tissue and blew her nose. "I . . . I belong to a theater group. Our director contacted Garrett Franklin about our using space in a building he owns. Wh-when Mr. Franklin found out I work here, he got awfully interested . . ."

Sam didn't have to listen to the rest of the story. She knew.

"And when I started to type the recipe, I knew I couldn't do it." Helen burst into tears. "My God, I nearly let myself get talked into committing a crime. What was I thinking of? What was Garrett thinking of?"

Sam knew exactly what Garrett had been thinking of. She patted Helen's shoulder. "There's no harm done. But you have to talk to my grandfather. He'll take care of the rest."

Helen's face paled. "Mr. Brewster will be furious."

"No, he'll be relieved."

Helen wrung her hands. "I don't know why I thought of such a thing. I felt trapped, wanting to help the theater company . . ."

"He'll understand," Sam assured her.

She sent Helen to repair her makeup and comb her hair, then ushered her into Clint's office and went back to work. She was disappointed that she hadn't found the original chili thief, but perhaps tonight they would.

They didn't, though Wade spent hours hunched over the keyboard, going through files and disks. Not only did they not discover who the thief was, the files gave them no clue as to who it *wasn't*.

Sam's eyelids drooped by the time Wade called it quits. He, too, looked exhausted. He ran a careless hand through his hair. "No luck."

Sam yawned. "What do we do?"

"Give me a day to think about it, then I'll tell you."

THE NEXT EVENING, as soon as it was dark, Wade slipped into Jerry Snow's apartment and began a systematic search. Fortunately, the place was small, with only one bedroom, and Snow didn't have much to look through.

The sparsely furnished living room yielded nothing, but the desk in the bedroom had one interesting item. A copy of *Terlingua Trails*, the CASI newsletter. "What a coincidence," Wade muttered sarcastically.

He finished in the bedroom and moved into the kitchen. This room must get a lot more use than the rest of the apartment, Wade thought. Cookbooks, one of them open to a recipe for stew, were piled on the table. Knives of various sizes hung over the counter and several bowls and a large stirring spoon sat in the dish drainer.

Wade noticed a manila folder on the counter. He opened it. Inside were three photocopies of a recipe: Hotter Than Hot Chili. *Bingo!*

"Mr. Snow," Wade murmured. "You and I are gonna have a meeting." He picked up the folder, quickly searched the rest of the kitchen, then left.

From his truck, he called Clint Brewster and told him the news.

"Give me the name and number of that fellow from CASI," Clint said. "I'll call and let him know we found the recipe in this Snow character's kitchen. When are you going to pick that bastard up?"

"This weekend," Wade said. "I know where to find him."

"Good. We've had production of our new chili on hold long enough. I want to get moving on it."

As soon as Clint hung up, Wade called Sam and filled her in. "It's time for a confrontation with Jerry Snow and the Hot Hombres. You'd better clear your calendar for the weekend. We're going to Terlingua."

10

Sam stood on the runway of Houston Executive Air at Hobby Airport. "Are you sure you know how to fly this thing?" she asked dubiously, eyeing the trim Cessna that belonged to Down Home Foods.

"I showed you my pilot's license last night," Wade said.

"I'm putting my life in your hands. I want you to remember that."

Wade grinned, enjoying the sight of her perfectly rounded bottom as she climbed into the small plane. He didn't mind a bit having her life in his hands. He liked being responsible for her, sharing with her, making love with her, even arguing with her.

He walked around and climbed into the pilot's seat, buckled his seat belt and checked the dials on the instrument panel. He radioed the tower for clearance. "Here we go," he said. "Next stop, Terlingua."

In the chili world, all trails led to Terlingua, Texas. The mecca of chilidom, the little town on the edge of Big Bend National Park hosted the International Chili Cook-off each fall. The rest of the year, Terlingua, population twenty-five, was a ghost town. Only during the chili cook-off did it come to life, when thousands of chili cooks and tasters converged on it from every corner of the United States and beyond.

Sam had worried that they'd never find a place to stay. After all, the Chihuahuan Desert wasn't overrun with hotels, but Wade had a contact in Alpine, not far from Terlingua, who'd invited them to stay with him. He'd also agreed to meet them at the airport and arrange for a rental car.

Halfway between Houston and San Antonio, Sam gestured to the ground below them. "Isn't Nick Petrelli's ranch somewhere down there?"

"In this area, but a little closer to Houston."

"How'd you come up with Nick?" Sam asked.

For a moment, Wade pondered her question. Nick had been part of his life for so long, he'd almost forgotten that he'd made the guy up. "I spent the summer working on a ranch after my first year of college. I met a lot of cowboys."

"And?"

"They're great storytellers. One of the guys I worked with was a stoop-shouldered, gray-haired ol' coot with the strength of a bull and a line of it to go along. We'd sit out under the stars after work at night and he'd tell me tall tales of cattle rustlers he'd outwitted, oilmen he'd outfoxed and some modern-day desperadoes he'd brought to justice. And of course, ladies he'd—"

"Charmed the pants off?"

"Yeah, according to him, his romantic exploits were legendary."

Sam laughed. "Like Nick's."

Wade decided not to mention the fact that lately Nick had begun thinking of curbing his lustful tendencies and settling down. This wasn't the time for such confidences, not when Nick *and* Wade still had a lot of thinking to do on that score. "Anyway," he continued, "when I started my first book, I figured I was up against tough competition. If I wanted to sell and sell big, my main character had to stand out."

"So you combined the P.I. with the cowboy and, presto, Nick Petrelli."

"Not quite that easily," Wade said, "but you got the general idea."

"How's Nick's latest adventure coming along?" Sam asked.

"Almost done."

"What's this one about?"

"The usual. Nick's after the bad guys."

"I'm sure your story's more original than that," Sam said.

"Nope. All mysteries deal with the struggle between right and wrong. Good versus evil. Order versus chaos."

"And yours, of course, have a dash of Nick's, or rather *your* homespun philosophy thrown in."

"Yep, I told you, Nick speaks for me."

"I wish you'd let me read the new one."

"I told you, Sam, no one sees my work un—"

"I know. Until it's on the shelves." She let out an exasperated sigh. "Did Marlene read your books?"

"She wasn't interested."

"But I am."

"Because you want to be sure you aren't in it."

She shook her head. "I'm interested because you wrote it."

Her words staggered him. Though they'd been together almost constantly in the past few weeks and had made love many times, this was the first time she'd said anything that gave him a clue to her feelings. He felt a tightness in his chest. If they'd been on the ground, he would have pulled her into his arms. He reached for her hand and raised it to his lips. "Maybe," he murmured. "Yeah, maybe."

He wondered what she'd think of Al McGuire. The character was no longer a blonde or a private eye—he'd changed her to an industrial psychologist—but she had a Samantha-like allure that kept Nick coming back again and again. He'd even spent an entire night with her. In the chapter Wade had just written—the next to last—Nick had begun thinking of asking Al to move in with him. A radical departure from the Nick Petrelli of past books, but Al had him so enthralled, Nick didn't want to give her up at the end of the book.

Man, he thought. *Nick's losing it, and so are you, Phillips.* Next thing he knew, he'd be shopping for rings. *Never,* he ordered himself, calling up the image of Marlene. Damn, the image of all the horrors married life entailed was becoming fuzzy.

SAM WAS TOUCHED by Wade's near capitulation. She'd begun to understand how important it was to him to keep his book private. But she really did want to read it, and she'd been as surprised as he was to realize that her reason had changed. She pondered that for a while. She cared about Wade, more than she should. Now that their mutual case was likely to end soon, she'd have to get used to the idea that their relationship would end, too. *Short-term.* Hadn't she gone along with that? And it would be just as they'd agreed, unless . . .

Unless she figured out a way to make it last. Why not? She could do anything she set her mind to. She'd give it some thought.

When they landed in Alpine early in the afternoon, Wade's friend strode out to greet them. He glanced around as if looking for someone, then shot Wade a puzzled frown.

Wade clapped him on the shoulder and shook his hand. "Sam Brewster, this is David Holloway, the pride of the National Park Service."

David looked like the classic outdoorsman. Tall and tanned, he had thick reddish blond hair streaked gold by the sun. His eyes were arresting, a deep and unusual shade of golden brown, and for a moment they studied Sam with quiet intensity. Then he chuckled and his golden eyes sparkled with laughter. He didn't explain what struck him as funny. Instead, he enveloped Sam's hand in his large, callused one. "Nice to meet you. Here, I'll take your bag."

Wade went to see where the plane would be housed, and Sam and David went inside the small terminal to wait for him. "Can I get you some coffee?" David asked.

"Yes, thanks."

He brought her a cup and one for himself, then stood smiling at her. "So you're Sam. To tell the truth, I'd pictured someone quite different."

"A man."

"Yeah." His eyes crinkled with amusement. Then he frowned again. "I thought Wade said he was here for the chili cook-off because he was working on a case."

"He is."

Before she could add that she was, too, Wade strolled up. "All set," he said.

David handed Wade a key ring. "Rental car and an extra key to my place." He gave Wade directions to his house and a map with the highway to Terlingua highlighted. "What are your plans?"

"We'll drive to Terlingua and scope out the cook-off this afternoon. Know where it is?"

"Which cook-off?" David said.

"The international championship."

"There are two of them."

"*Two* championships? The guy from CASI didn't say anything about another one."

"Of course not. Political infighting. CASI split off from the original group, but they still hold the championships at the same time. CASI's is the big one. It's at Rancho de CASI, a couple of miles past Terlingua on your right. How long will you be there?"

"Couple of hours at most," Wade said. "We're not planning to nail these guys till tomorrow."

"Then why don't I drive down and meet you for dinner later?" David said. "We'll eat at La Kiva. It's on the banks of

Terlingua Creek as you head back from the cook-off. It's famous around these parts. You don't want to miss it."

"Sure," Wade said. "Thanks for all your help. See you later." He took Sam's bag and they left the terminal and found the van David had arranged for them.

A shiver of both excitement and fear skittered up Sam's spine as they drove away from the airport. The climax of her first case. "Shouldn't we check with Buck Stapleton when we get to the cook-off? Won't he know where the Hombres are?"

"When I called him, he said no. They don't have assigned spaces. People cook at their campsites," Wade replied. "Now, let's go over the plan one more time. We get a bead on the Hombres today. Then tomorrow, when they take their chili to the judges, Stapleton will have a couple of police officers ready to escort them off the grounds."

Sam nodded. "And when they're out of the way, we corner Snow, question him, then turn him in, too. You didn't tell Stapleton about him, did you?"

Wade shook his head. "I wanted to be sure we had time to talk to him before the police take over. We'll explain that to Stapleton afterward."

"Okay, but if he calls me little lady one more time, the police may have to haul *me* in, too. For assault and battery."

They headed south toward Big Bend National Park. Mountains flanked them, brown and rugged against an aquamarine sky. A hawk sailed overhead as they cruised along. Sam stared out the window at the stark landscape. "I bet this area hasn't changed for centuries."

Wade nodded. "The Indians who used to ride through the Chisos Mountains would probably still recognize them today. Nothing around but prickly pear and cholla, not many animals, either."

Sam itched to get out her camera and have Wade pull over, but she knew they needed to get to work. Someday, she'd—

they'd, she corrected herself optimistically—come back and explore.

They almost missed Terlingua. A true ghost town with crumbling adobe houses and a stone church, it clung to the red slope of a mountain. They passed a deserted cemetery with graves marked by stone crosses. The lack of flowers spoke eloquently of the loneliness of desert life and death.

A few miles farther on, they spotted the entrance to Rancho de CASI, and followed a lone pickup truck inside. A friendly red-faced man took their admission fee and directed them to the visitors' parking area at the top of the incline ahead.

"Would you look at that!" Sam said when they got out of the van.

Fresh from the isolation of the desert, they'd come upon a sprawling settlement. Below them in a rocky basin were cars, vans, RVs, dirt bikes. Hundreds, maybe thousands. People in bright-colored Western clothes milled around, waving, shouting, hugging. Sounds of laughter and country music soared upward.

"Welcome to Chiliville," Wade murmured.

They clambered down the slope past a huge rock chiseled in the shape of a chili pepper and painted red, then found themselves in the midst of a noisy group in chili garb. T-shirts, caps, earrings, scarves—everything had a chili motif. "Where are you all from?" Wade asked.

"West Virginia."

"That far?"

"Oh, sure," one of the women said. "There are folks here from Canada, Wisconsin, even the Virgin Islands."

"Let's start looking," Wade said to Sam as the group moved on. "Put on your sunglasses. No use letting the Hombres get another look at you."

"You think they'll remember me?"

"Trust me, Samantha. No one who's seen you could forget you."

Sam pulled a scarf from her jacket pocket and tied it around her head. What if the Hombres did recognize her even with her sunglasses and scarf on? They'd handle whatever arose—correction, *she'd* handle it. This was what being a detective was all about. She slipped on her glasses, and they began a systematic search of the grounds.

They wandered along dozens of rows of vehicles, with no luck. They saw people already cooking pots of chili, others lounging on folding chairs. A group of kids was playing softball along the edge of the settlement. At the end of one row, a gang of grown-up kids was hanging a banner advertising a wet T-shirt contest, while a couple of them rode motorcycles in a circle, kicking up dust.

Past the motorcycle maniacs, they turned onto the next row, and Sam pulled up short. "There!" Her heart began a slow thud. "See those fellows in the matching shirts?"

Wade narrowed his eyes. "They haven't seen me before. I'll take a look. You stay over here and take pictures."

"Okay."

"Don't be too obvious about it," he warned.

Sam got out her camera and a telephoto lens. Wade sauntered down the row of vehicles, stopped to visit with a shaggy-bearded man stirring a kettle of chili, then moved on. He halted by the men Sam had pointed out. They were sitting on camp stools, listening to country music on a portable radio. Suddenly, she wondered if he planned to apprehend the Hombres now.

He'd better not. That wasn't part of the plan.

Or maybe she didn't know the plan. Maybe he hadn't told her.

She started forward. A roar sounded in her ears. A gun? She whirled.

No, a motorcycle. Like a demon from hell, it barreled straight toward her. Sam jumped back. She heard a scream. Her own.

Hand over her heart, she leaned against someone's truck and shut her eyes.

"Miss, are you okay?"

The voice made her jump again. She opened her eyes. A small crowd had gathered around her. A tall, bronzed man stood beside her. "Wh-what?" she mumbled.

"He almost ran you down."

"Didn't even stop," someone observed.

"You look mighty pale," the man continued. "Are you okay?"

"Yes, I'm fine."

"What the heck were you doing?" growled a familiar voice at her other side.

She turned. Wade's eyes were dark and angry, but his face was dead white. A muscle jumped in his cheek. *He's scared,* Sam thought. "I'm fine," she repeated, ignoring his question.

His jaw clenched. "Good. Don't do that again." He turned and stared in the direction the motorcycle had gone. "Was that Jerry Snow?"

"I don't know." She hadn't had time to get a look at the man as he sped by.

"I'm betting it was. When I get hold of him tomorrow, I'll—" He muttered something unprintable.

Sam brushed the dust from her jacket. As furious as Wade was, she supposed he could have said a lot more. Well, she wasn't too calm herself. She wondered if the driver *had* been Snow and felt a shudder race down her spine. She swallowed tears that threatened and forced herself to speak in a normal tone. "You talked to the Hombres. What about?"

"I asked if they'd entered the contest, and they have. They told me tomorrow's schedule." He had apparently tamped down his emotions, too, for he gave her a half smile. "Nice of them, huh? We know just what time to show up."

"Where'd they go?" she asked, glancing toward their space.

"To buy themselves a beer. Come on. Let's get out of here."

They trudged back to the parking area and drove away from the CASI enclave. When they reached La Kiva, Sam said, "Give me the keys. I think I'll skip dinner."

Wade frowned. "Are you okay? The motorcycle didn't hit you, did it?"

"Of course not. I'm just not hungry."

A tap on the window got their attention. David stood by the car. Wade rolled down his window. "Sorry you made the trip, buddy. Sam doesn't feel like dinner."

"But you two go ahead," she said. "You can catch up on old times." Wade looked doubtful. "Go on," she insisted. "If David will give me directions to his house, I'll see you all later."

After David had done so and had told her to make herself at home, Wade got out of the car and Sam sighed with relief. She was tired and dusty and still shaky from her experience with the motorcycle. She didn't want to spend the evening listening to the men reminisce. What she craved was a hot shower and a soft bed, and the way she felt now, she wasn't interested in sharing either of them.

AS WADE STARED after the van, he was aware of David watching him with interest.

"So who's Sam?" the park ranger asked.

Wade kicked at a rock. "She's a pain in the butt."

"Yeah, pal. I can see that she would be. Man, the woman is ugly as sin."

"Okay, laugh all you want to, but you don't have to deal with her. She wants to be a private detective."

David halted in the middle of the parking lot. "Have you taken her on as a partner?"

"No way." He explained the situation.

David nodded. "I didn't think you'd want another partner. Still, as temporary help goes, the lady sure is easy on the eyes."

"And I didn't think *you* were eyeing women again."

David's expression turned stony. "I'm not."

They entered the restaurant via a steep flight of steps. The tables in the small dining rooms were polished redwood stumps; the chairs, too, were carved from stumps and trimmed with cowhide. Dim recessed lights along the walls illuminated the rooms with a mysterious glow.

"Let's sit outside," David suggested, and they found a table on the wide stone patio where a rock band played. They ordered barbecue, which was tender and delicious, and brought each other up-to-date on their lives.

Wade outlined the case, and David chuckled. "The great chili caper," he said.

David, who had resigned from the Houston Police Department after his wife, also a cop, was gunned down by a juvenile gang, talked about the peace he'd found in his job as a park ranger.

"Think you'll ever come back?" Wade asked.

"Never."

They talked about mutual friends, lingered over their beer, but as the evening wore on, Wade began surreptitiously checking his watch.

"Worried about her?" David asked.

Wade sighed. He thought he'd concealed his agitation, but David was a perceptive guy. "Yeah," he admitted. Being with David, remembering his friend's tragedy, made him think how easily something could have happened to Sam this afternoon. "Mind if we leave?"

They drove back to Alpine beneath a vast black sky. The heavens seemed higher here, the stars brighter. The land was as beautiful as it was harsh. But Wade couldn't appreciate the landscape. His mind was on Samantha. Even though she'd insisted she was all right, he needed to reassure himself.

Inside the house, he refused another beer and excused himself, explaining that they needed to get up early. He and David both knew that wasn't the real reason. He wanted to be with Sam.

He found her already asleep, one arm stretched across the pillow. He undressed quietly so as not to disturb her—they really did need to get an early start—but he couldn't resist sitting on the edge of the bed and looking at her as she slept. A lock of hair lay over her cheek. Gently, he brushed it back, then bent to plant a whisper-soft kiss in its place.

SAM'S EYES OPENED and she stared drowsily at Wade. "When'd you get here?" she mumbled.

"A few minutes ago. I didn't mean to wake you."

"'S all right."

"Is it?" His voice was deep, his eyes blue-black.

"Uh-huh."

He leaned closer, framing her face with his hands and gazing into her eyes. "Are you okay?"

She shivered, remembering the terror she'd felt seeing the motorcycle bearing down on her.

Then Wade kissed her and she didn't want to remember, didn't need to think of anything else. She lifted the sheet and he slipped into bed beside her, and made love to her as he'd never done before. Always they'd been consumed by each other. Their lovemaking had been wild and primitive, but not tonight.

Tonight, he touched her as if she was precious, his fingers flowing across her skin, his lips brushing hers ever so gently. He kissed her slowly, tenderly, aroused her with such infinite patience that Sam floated over the edge almost without realizing it. Afterward, he held her against his chest and she fell asleep listening to the steady beat of his heart against her ear.

WADE SLEPT POORLY. Usually, he didn't worry over his cases, but this one was an exception. Because of Sam. He wished he could think of a way to keep her here in Alpine, but he knew she'd never agree to that. Maybe, with luck, they'd corner the chili thieves without incident.

They ate a quick breakfast and silently retraced their route to the cook-off. When they arrived at the already crowded parking area, Wade said, "Remember, we don't do anything until they head for the judging area." He checked his watch. "According to the schedule they gave me yesterday, that'll be in about an hour. Want to watch the showmanship events while we wait?"

"Sure." To liven up the cook-off, teams of cooks could compete in the showmanship events by singing, dancing or just plain acting silly. Sam and Wade wandered over to watch the Hot Cha-Chas, three men in blond wigs, painted faces and garish costumes doing a clumsy but enthusiastic version of the Latin dance. Next to them, a woman and a white poodle danced to "How Much is That Doggie in the Window?" Nearby, a group enacted an old-fashioned melodrama, complete with mustachioed villain and gesticulating heroine.

"Enjoying yourself?" Wade asked.

Sam shook her head. "All the acts are cute, but I can't appreciate them. I'm thinking about . . ."

"Yeah, I know. Let's have some chili. Maybe that'll get your mind on something else."

"Chili? Hardly." But when he bought two sampling cups, she accepted one. They tried some of the showmanship entrants' offerings. "None of it's as good as Granddad's," Sam said.

After they'd had enough showmanship, they strolled over to the booths with items for sale. Wade bought Sam an official cook-off poster. "So you'll have something to remember this by."

Sam laughed. "I doubt I'll ever forget, but thanks."

Fifteen minutes before judging time for the Hombres, Wade and Sam checked with Buck Stapleton, who summoned a police officer. Wade and Stapleton joined the uniformed lawman at the entrance to the judging area and Sam stood nearby, camera ready to record the Hombres' ouster.

Right on time, Hank and Billy Joe ambled up. They were wearing matching cook-off T-shirts and their faces sported identical grins, which disappeared when a hand barred their way into the arena.

Sam, standing a little ways off, snapped a picture as the police officer growled, "Hank Sterling?"

"Y-yes, sir."

"You can't bring that chili in for judging."

Hank rummaged in his pocket. "It says right here, two-thirty. See?"

"Doesn't matter what that paper says. You're disqualified."

"But . . . but why?"

"Using a stolen recipe."

What appeared to be genuine confusion flashed across Hank's face. "Stolen? Me and Billy here, we don't know anything about stolen. We didn't steal nothing."

"No, sir," his brother chimed in. "We didn't steal it. We don't know nothin' about chili. We don't even know anything about cookin'."

Hank nodded vigorously. "The guy that hired us musta done it."

"Yeah," Billy Joe agreed. "Snow musta stole it."

Buck Stapleton spoke up. "Who stole it doesn't matter. You'll have to leave."

The Sterling brothers stared at each other in dismay. Sam took another shot.

"The officer will escort you off the grounds," Stapleton continued.

Looking dazed, the Hombres—the *ex*-Hombres, Wade corrected himself—fell into step beside the policeman.

Wade nodded in approval, shook Stapleton's hand and walked over to Sam. "Step one completed. Now, let's go talk to Snow." They turned and started for the Hombres' space. "Once we get there, I'll—"

"Wade!" Sam grabbed his arm. "There he is."

At the other end of the line of cars stood Snow, shading his eyes against the sun. He stared at the cop marching the Hombres out the entrance and away from the cook-off. Then he ran.

"Damn!" Wade dashed after Snow as the man bolted for the ridge. "He's got a twenty-yard head start." Over his shoulder, he shouted, "Get a cop, Sam."

Instead, Sam yelled at a bystander. "You heard what he said. Get the police."

Behind him, Wade heard footsteps crunching on gravel. The cop? He glanced over his shoulder. No, damn it. Sam! Camera in hand, she raced after him.

11

"GO BACK!" Wade shouted.

Sam kept coming.

No use wasting his breath. Stubborn woman would follow him if she wanted to. He concentrated on Snow. The man ran up the incline and dodged between a pickup and a van. Wade followed, gaining only inches.

Snow tripped and slowed. Wade sped up, but a car pulled out in front of him. It barred his way, cut off his line of vision for a moment. He swerved around it, saw Snow again. *Faster,* he ordered himself.

People stopped to stare. A woman screamed as Snow passed her, almost knocking her down. A dog yapped, jerked free of its owner and ran after Snow. The owner joined the chase.

Snow was fast, but the dog was faster. Near the edge of the parking area, it caught up with him and grabbed his pant leg. Wrenching free, Snow leaped up on the fender of a new Chevy. He turned and Wade heard him bellow, "Get away, you rotten creep."

Wade ran up and slid to a halt. The dog, a feisty little mutt, had the situation well in hand. It gazed up at Snow, curled its lip and growled.

Snow cursed and crawled across the hood. Wade lunged, grabbed him and wrestled him down. The dog pranced in front of the car, barking excitedly.

"Caesar!" Puffing, the dog's owner rushed up. "Leave that man alone!"

Caesar glanced sideways at his red-faced master, pawed the ground and let out another growl. The man bent to snap the animal's leash on. "I'm sor—"

With the dog captured, Snow tried to twist out of Wade's grasp.

"The cops'll be here in a second," Wade panted. "Don't move."

"The hell with that." Snow's boot slammed into Wade's thigh, and his hold loosened. It was all Snow needed. He jerked away.

"Hold it. I've got a gun."

As shocked as Snow appeared to be, Wade turned toward the voice. Sam stood on the opposite side of the car, her hand grasping something in her pocket.

Caesar's owner yanked the leash and backed away. Wade pinned Snow to the car.

"That ain't no gun," Snow snorted.

Sam smiled. "No? Try me and you'll find out."

Snow stopped struggling.

"Good," Wade said. "I have some questions for you while we're waiting for the cops. How'd you get your hands on the chili recipe?"

Snow swore. "Oh, man. I didn't take it. I was just the middleman."

"So what was your job?"

"I hired the cooks. Hell, man, they weren't even cooks. All they did was heat the stuff. But listen, you gotta believe me," he whined. "I didn't know that recipe was stolen."

"No?"

"No. Hey, I got a rap sheet a yard long. Why would I wanna get mixed up stealin'? I didn't know anything about this."

Sam stepped closer. "You knocked me down in Flatonia. Why'd you do that if you didn't know what was going on?"

"Hank said you were askin' questions. Guy that hired me told me to be careful, someone might try to steal the recipe. Hey, I didn't hurt you none, just bumped you a little."

"And yesterday, when you tried to run me down with your motorcycle? What about that?"

Snow looked confused. "I don't know what you're talking about. I didn't try to run anybody down."

Wade frowned. Snow might be off the hook for the motorcycle incident, but just bumping Sam "a little" in Flatonia was still too much. He gave Snow a shake. "Who hired you?"

"Think I'd tell you that? You crazy or somethin'?"

"I think you'd be damn smart to tell me," Wade said. "With your record, you ought to try to be as cooperative as you can."

Snow pondered that for a minute. Finally, he said, "I met him through a computer bulletin board. He sent me an E-mail, said he'd checked me out and wanted me to do some work for him. Said he needed someone to handle his chili for him because he was too busy. Hell, it sounded legal and the pay was good."

"Legal, huh?" Wade snorted. "Then why did the Hombres register for the cook-offs under assumed names?"

Snow shrugged. "The guy said it was a precaution. What did I know?"

"You know the guy's *name*."

"Yeah, but look, I don't want to rat on him."

Before Wade could point out that Snow's loyalty was misplaced, two police officers ran up. "Guy who came and got me wasn't sure which way you'd gone," one of them panted. "What's the problem?"

Quickly, Wade explained and within minutes the officers led Jerry Snow away. Wade waited until they were out of sight, then turned to Sam. "What on God's green earth made you follow me? You could have gotten yourself—" He caught himself. "You could have gotten hurt."

Her chin shot up. "So could you. Anyway, I didn't. You needed me. I got him to be still, didn't I?"

"Yeah," he admitted, then shook his head. "Do you really have a gun?"

She laughed. "Uh-uh. A hairbrush."

Wade pulled her close for a quick kiss. "Sam Brewster, you're something else. Come on, let's go back to the Hombres' space. Snow's computer wasn't in his apartment in Houston. Let's see if he brought it with him."

They trudged back. To their relief, the Hombres' RV was unlocked. A laptop computer lay on one of the seats. "Finding what we want could take a while," Wade said. "We'll take it with us. I doubt Snow will need it where he's going."

"We should talk to Stapleton before we leave," Sam remarked.

They found him at the judging booth. He listened to the account of Jerry Snow's capture and said, "You'll get an official letter from CASI, but I want to say thank you in person. You've saved us a lot of embarrassment." He shook Wade's hand, then turned to Sam. "Thank you, too, little lady."

Sam waited until he walked off, then muttered, "You're welcome, little man."

Back at David's house, they plugged in the computer and began going through Snow's files. Finally, after about three hours, they found what they were looking for. An E-mail letter asking for a meeting with Snow and signed—

"Richard Merchant," Wade read.

"I can't believe it," Sam said. "Richard's not smart enough for corporate espionage, especially when it involves breaking into computer files. He must've had help."

"On the inside," Wade agreed.

"But who?"

"We'll find that out from Richard."

THE NEXT DAY, they went straight from Hobby Airport to Richard's house. Located in a pricey development along Buffalo Bayou, it looked like a Gothic castle. Sam didn't care for Gothic castles, but then, she didn't care much for Richard, either. "I bet it has a large kitchen," she muttered.

They rang the bell and Richard, dressed in T-shirt and running shorts, opened the door. "Samantha and, um, Phillips. What a surprise." That seemed an understatement; he looked flabbergasted. "Come in, come in," he said in a weak attempt at joviality.

He led them into the living room where a football game blared on the TV. The remains of a large pizza sat on the coffee table. "What can I get you?" Richard asked. "Beer? Wi—"

"No need to be cordial," Wade said, blocking the doorway. "We're here on business. About a chili recipe stolen from Down Home Foods."

A slow flush spread from Richard's throat upward, but he tried to appear confused. "I don't understand."

"Sure you do," Sam put in pleasantly, "since you're behind it."

"Now, wait a minute," Richard sputtered, clenching his fists. "You two can't walk in here and . . . and . . ."

Wade smiled at him. "And accuse you of masterminding the theft? Of course we can."

By now, Richard's face had turned crimson. "Who do you think you are, Phillips?"

"I'm a private investigator. Clint Brewster hired me to track down the chili thief. Which I've done."

"But . . . but how did you . . ."

"Richard, I get to ask the questions. How did *you*?"

"You'll never know that." Like a football lineman, Richard lunged and knocked Wade to the floor. Then he darted out the door.

"Oh, my God!" Sam screamed. Wade lay on the floor, stunned. She crouched beside him. "Wade! Wade, open your eyes." He didn't move. "Water," she muttered and ran into the kitchen. She grabbed a dish towel from the counter, wet it and ran back to the living room.

By now, Wade had managed to sit up and lean against the wall. He rubbed his jaw. "Man, that guy packs a punch."

Sam knelt at his side, her hands shaking as she ran them over his face. "Where are you hurt?"

He sucked in his breath. "Jaw, but I'll live. Which way did he go?"

"I . . . I don't know. I heard the car start." Wade got to his feet. "You can't go after him," Sam cried. "You're—" She grabbed his arm. "I'll drive."

Wade struggled to his feet. "No, you won't. Don't give me any grief this time, Sam. See if this neighborhood has a security service. If it does, call them. If not, call the police." He opened the door and dashed out.

Sam started after him. No, she'd better call security. She waited a moment, standing in the doorway and watching as Wade took off like a race-car driver. "Be careful," she whispered. "Please be careful."

She hurried into the kitchen and sat at Richard's desk. A sticker on the phone provided the security service's number. Sam's hands shook as she punched the number into the phone; her voice shook as she gave Richard's address and explained the situation.

She hung up and squeezed her eyes shut. Why hadn't she insisted on going with Wade? He was already hurt. He could pass out and have an accident, get himself killed.

"Calm down," she told herself. "Think of something . . . anything."

She glanced around Richard's kitchen and turned up her nose in disgust. Dirty dishes cluttered the sink and counters. A carton of melting ice cream stood on the counter next to the refrigerator. She noticed a gummy mess on the floor by the sink. "Pigsty," she muttered, turning back to the desk. A calendar from September hung on the wall above it. Old newspapers and mail lay on it in haphazard piles.

Maybe she should check Richard's correspondence. She might find something to connect him to Down Home Foods. She pawed through the mess on the desk but got up every few minutes to dash to the window and look out. Meanwhile, on the desk she saw nothing except bills, circulars, girlie magazines and out-of-date newspapers.

Someone pounded on the front door. Sam ran to it, looked out and saw two constables. "Thank God," she cried, throwing open the door.

"You got a disturbance here?" one of them asked.

"We did. The man got away and my friend went after him." She pointed down the street and the constables dashed back to their car.

Now what? She could go through the house and look for evidence of Richard's involvement in the theft. *Yes,* she decided, and she ought to take notes. She rifled through the papers on Richard's desk until she found a notepad. Then she grabbed a pencil from a mug decorated with a crest, but her hands shook so badly that she knocked the mug to the floor and broke it. "Oh, great." She bent to gather up the scattered pencils and pieces of china, then threw the shards in the heaping garbage can. Richard would have to do without the memento, whatever it was.

Notepad in hand, Sam wandered through the house, but she couldn't concentrate. Ten more minutes passed, then the doorbell rang. "Sam, open up," Wade called.

She dashed to open the door. Wade shoved Richard inside.

Richard stumbled into the living room, slid to the floor and sat, holding his head and looking dazed.

Sam stared from one to the other. Wade's face was pale and bruised, his nose was bloody. "Wh-what happened?" she asked.

Wade chuckled, then grimaced with pain. "I found him right away. He'd driven a couple of blocks, then he apparently lost control of his car and crashed into a portable sign in someone's yard. When I got there, he'd passed out."

"Then what took you so long?"

"Dragging him to my car. He was deadweight. Then the homeowner came out and started yelling about the sign. The crash rearranged all the letters. The message changed from Lordy, Lordy, Janice Turned Forty to Janice Rotted." He chuckled, grimaced again. "Janice was not amused. Neither was her husband. I had to fix it."

"And Richard just sat in your car all that time?"

"Dazed. The same way he's sitting now."

They both turned and glanced at Richard. He looked like a beached whale.

"Should we find something to tie him up with?" Sam asked.

"Nah, I think he's harmless."

"I'll call the constables' switchboard and tell them you're back," Sam said.

"Uh-uh." Wade motioned Sam to follow him into the kitchen. "As long as we're by ourselves, let's ask him a few questions first."

"Do you think he'll answer them without a lawyer here?"

"Honey, as muddled as he is, he probably will. Even under the best of circumstances, old Rich may not think about the importance of having counsel present. Let's give it a try."

They returned to the living room, and Wade sat down across from Richard. "While we're waiting for the police, we have some questions for you."

Richard shook his head slowly. "I don't have to tell you anything."

"We already know most of it," Wade said. "We went through Jerry Snow's files."

Richard's face turned dead white.

"Thought that would impress you. You want to tell us the rest? Like how you broke into Down Home's files?"

"I didn't break into any files," Richard said.

"No? I didn't think so," Wade said. "Who'd you get to do it for you?"

Richard managed a half snort. "Figure it out on your own. You think I'd betray a brother?"

Sam gaped at him. "Your brother did it?" She couldn't believe Drew, the consummate playboy, had the inclination or the skills to indulge in computer piracy.

"Not Drew. He knew about it, but he was off in Hollywood or Monte Carlo or somewhere."

Just as she'd thought. "So who—"

"I'm not gonna tell you, I said."

"Tell us *why* you did it, then," Sam said. She walked around to stand in front of him.

He gazed up at her, his pale blue eyes sincere. "For my grandfather."

Sam drew a breath. "Surely Jake wouldn't ask you to do something like that."

"No, he didn't ask me. I thought it up on my own." Richard's voice was that of a little boy, pleased with his exploits.

"But why?" Sam crouched beside him...but not too close. Even though he was groggy, she didn't want to get near those muscles, especially since she'd seen evidence of the damage he could do when he'd tackled Wade.

"To show him I could do something for the company," he said as if it were the most obvious reason imaginable.

"But—"

"*He* never made a chili. *I* wanted to do it."

"But, Richard," Sam said, "you stole it."

"No one would've known if . . . if . . . How did you find out the recipe was taken? Did he tell?"

"Who?" Wade asked.

"My. . . friend. No, he wouldn't rat on me."

"Clint found out when he judged a cook-off," Sam said. "If you hadn't entered the chili, he would never have known."

"Damn!" Richard muttered. "I wanted it to be a championship recipe."

"It nearly was," Sam said. "It was good."

Richard sighed and rubbed his temple. "Hurts," he muttered and shut his eyes.

Wade got up slowly as if he hurt, too, and beckoned to Sam. "You might as well call the police now. We've found out all we're going to."

She did and within a few minutes, the officers arrived. Wade reported the incident and told them he and Sam would follow them down to the nearest police station and file charges.

It took both officers to haul Richard onto his feet. "Hey," he said as they marched him toward the door, "can I take a soda with me? I'm thirsty."

"No," one of the officers said. "Let's get going."

Sam watched, bemused, as they led Richard away, then she and Wade went to their car. "Let me drive," she said. "You can use a rest."

"Yeah." Wade got in the passenger side, shut his eyes and leaned back.

Instead of starting the car, Sam sat still and glanced at him with concern. Blood had dried on his cheeks and chin. His jaw had begun to turn purple. "Maybe I should take you home."

"I'm okay."

"I was worried about you," she said softly.

His eyes opened and he gave her a puzzled glance. "Why?"

Sam shook her head, surprised he'd have to ask. "Richard's as big as a tank. He could take on two or even three men, and you were alone. Of course I was worried. In fact, I was scared."

"You had no reason. Handling Richard was no problem."

"You conceited, macho male! I worried for the same reason you worry about me when I go off alone. Think about it." She gunned the engine and started after the patrol car.

She'd worried because... because she cared about him. She'd... oh, Lord, she'd fallen in love with him.

The thought, as simple as that, hit her with the force of an exploding rocket. She could barely drive as the idea swirled around in her mind. She was in love! She supposed she had been for a while, but she hadn't let the thought surface. Now that it had, she wanted to laugh and cry at the same time. This man—this *exasperating* man who teased her and loved her and tried too hard to protect her—was the one she'd been waiting for all her life.

He cared for her, too. She knew it, or why would he waste *his* time and energy worrying about her? She'd been insulted, she'd interpreted his anxiety as a sign he thought she was incompetent, but maybe it was a sign he cared. More than he realized.

She'd have to make him realize—Mr. In-for-the-Short-Term. It would take some doing. For starters, what if she convinced him they should work together? Once they were partners in business, he'd realize the partnership could be personal, as well. She glanced at him out of the corner of her eye. He stared back, a strange, pensive look on his face.

Sam braked as the stoplight ahead of them turned yellow. Wade gasped at the quick stop. "What's wrong?" Sam cried.

"My chest is a little sore. It's nothing."

"Nothing! A tank plowed into you and you say it's nothing." She glared at him. "As soon as we're finished at the police station, I'm taking you to the emergency room."

"Nah. I don't need—"

"Shut up, Phillips," she said and heard her voice tremble. "You need a doctor and I'm going to see that you get one."

As soon as they finished at the police station, Sam drove to the nearest hospital. Wade did indeed need a doctor. He had two broken ribs. After the doctor taped them, cleaned his bloody but unbroken nose and treated assorted scrapes and bruises, Sam drove him to her place.

"We need to talk to your grandfather," Wade said.

"I'll talk to him later. Right now, I'm going to take care of you," she said, unlocking the door. "You need a bath and bed. Get undressed."

"I can't take a bath with this tape on."

"You won't have to. I'll sponge you off. Come on." In the bathroom, she unbuttoned his shirt and slipped it off, then helped him remove the rest of his clothes. When he was stripped down to his shorts, she ordered him to sit, then began to bathe him. "Poor baby," she murmured as she sponged his face, "he really got you. Does it hurt?"

"Uh-uh." But his tone lacked conviction.

Sam kept her touch gentle as she cleaned his arms and chest. Just looking at his bruises made her ache.

When she finished the bath, she smoothed back his hair. He looked up at her with the same expression he'd worn in the car. "You're sweet, Samantha," he murmured.

"And you're tired. I'm going to fix you a bowl of soup, and then you're going to sleep."

"I'm fine," he protested, but she saw him wince as he got to his feet.

"Go to bed, Wade."

He was half-asleep when she brought him the soup, but he ate it hungrily. When he finished, she said, "The doctor gave me some pain pills for you."

"Oh, please!"

"I know, the great detective doesn't think he needs pain pills, but you're taking them, anyway. Open your mouth." Before he could say anything, she popped one in. "Here, swallow." She handed him a glass of water, then, satisfied that he'd swallowed the pills, put the glass on the night table. She bent to touch her lips to his. "My hero," she whispered.

Wade's eyes were dark and sleepy. "I'm not a hero, Sam," he murmured.

"Sure you are," she said and brushed a hand down his cheek. "I'm going to talk to Clint now. Get some sleep."

Wade shut his eyes as she closed the door. He should have gone along with her to talk to Brewster, but he felt pretty groggy. And he hurt.

He lay still, letting the pills work their magic, and thought about Samantha. Marlene had never worried about him. Sam had. At first, he'd been annoyed with Sam's overconcern...just the way she was when *he* worried about *her*. Yeah, now he could understand how that made *her* feel.

Then later, when she'd cared for him so sweetly, he'd found he didn't mind much at all. She had such a soft, gentle touch.

Maybe his old ideas about marriage were wrong, after all. Maybe with Sam . . .

But he still didn't want her working with him.

She wouldn't like that. A thought occurred to him. He could have her do photography for him every now and then, the way she'd done for the P.I. in Dallas. Yeah, that would keep her happy. He'd talk to her about it . . . soon . . .

THE NEXT MORNING, he felt stiff and sore, but he managed to hide his discomfort as he sat down across from Sam at the breakfast table. "How do you feel?" she asked.

"After all your care, I'm fine," he said, hoping he sounded more energetic than he felt. "What did Clint say when you told him about Richard?"

"He wasn't happy, of course, but he was relieved that Jake knew nothing. I told him I wasn't so sure that Jake had nothing to do with this, but he was. He said something interesting. Said they'd been bitter rivals all these years, hated each other's guts, but they'd never resorted to dirty dealings."

"Too bad Richard had to spoil things. Did Clint have any ideas about who might have given Richard the recipe?"

Sam shook her head. "And neither do I. At least we know it's a man. Richard referred to the person as 'he.'"

"Yeah, we've eliminated fifty percent of the population right there," Wade said wryly, "and twenty-five percent of those who had access to Ray Donovan's login and password."

"That rules out Lana Harvey," Sam agreed.

Wade nodded. "We'll figure it out."

"Yeah, we will. We work well together, don't we?"

Wade eyed her warily. He didn't want to get her hopes up about their becoming colleagues, but she deserved some praise. "Sure," he said. "If you hadn't taken those pictures in Flatonia, we might never have found the connection between the Sterling brothers and Jerry Snow." Sam smiled, and, encouraged, he continued, "You're a good photographer."

Her smile disappeared, but he plunged ahead, "All kinds of opportunities come up for photographers to work with P.I.s. You could, um, start a consulting firm. I could almost guarantee that within a couple of months you'd be as busy as you wanted . . .".

"*If* I wanted," she muttered, then glared at him. "What are you saying, Wade? That all I contributed to this case was a few pictures? That I belong in a photography studio, not a detective's office?" She shoved her breakfast away and to Wade's horror, her eyes filled with tears. "That's not what I want, damn it."

"Sam." He got up, came around to her and put his hand on her shoulder.

She brushed it off. "Go away."

"No," he said, tightening his grasp. "I'm not saying this to hurt you."

She sniffed. "But you are."

"Sam, yesterday you worried about me. I worry about you, too, you know that. Because I . . . I care about you."

Slowly, she turned and looked up at him. "You do?"

"Very much."

"Then don't—please don't—interfere with my dreams."

"Sam," he said heavily. "I don't know if I can—"

"Don't say anything else, Wade. I have to be at work early this morning. Let's talk about this tonight when we have time."

"Not tonight," he said with reluctance. "I'm meeting with a client."

"Tomorrow evening then."

"Sure," Wade said. He dropped a kiss on her cheek. "Bye, darlin'."

"Bye," Sam murmured. She listened to his footsteps crossing the living room. The front door slammed.

She didn't know what to think. He said he cared about her, but what did he mean by that? If he did care, really care, he'd respect her enough to let her go her own way. No, *want* her to. Instead, he thought she belonged in a photography studio, did he? Her mood turned angry. And after all she'd accomplished on this case! Found out what Garrett Franklin was up to, gotten Jerry Snow out into the open in Flatonia, tricked him into thinking she had a gun. Why, without her, Wade wouldn't be anywhere near to solving the case. "Ungrateful . . ." She was angry enough that she couldn't think of an ungrateful *what*.

She picked up her plate and Wade's and stomped to the dishwasher to put them inside. She'd show him. She'd figure out who had broken into the files, and she'd do it before Wade even had a clue. She slammed the dishwasher shut. If only she could figure out a connection between Richard and someone in the firm . . .

For the rest of the morning, as she drove to the office and went about her work, she racked her brain. As far as she knew, Richard didn't socialize with anyone in the Down Home organization. Had they ever hired someone who'd worked at Tru-Tex? Had Richard planted a spy?

That was a thought. After lunch, she went to personnel and asked for the files of the three men who might have broken into the computer. All had been here for some time and none had worked for the Merchants' company. On the other hand, they might have neglected to mention that they'd been employed by a competitor.

She read their backgrounds. Two of them had grown up in Houston. Only Keith came from out of state—California. He'd attended the University of Arizona, the other two men had graduated from the University of Texas. All had good references from past jobs and good reviews here.

Finally, Sam put away the folders and went back upstairs. The afternoon wore on. Helen stopped in to tell her how relieved she was to have cleared her conscience. "Mr. Brewster said he'd deal with Garrett," she said.

"I'm sure he'll handle it so that you're not involved," Sam assured her.

When Helen left, Sam sat tapping her pencil on the desk. Something had begun to nag her, but she couldn't put her finger on it. Something Richard had said? Something she'd seen in his house? Just out of reach, it tantalized her, but she couldn't grab on to it.

When she got home, she changed clothes and prepared to do her yoga exercises. She'd been neglecting her regimen lately; her nerves showed it. She needed to center herself; she needed to relax. She was glad Wade was tied up this evening. Hurt and anger still festered inside her after his remark this morning. She turned on her tape player, lay down and concentrated on breathing slowly and deeply.

Deeper and deeper her mind went. To a place of tranquillity, of light, a place where she was open to healing energy. Deeper, farther.

When she'd finished her exercise, she sat up slowly. The tension had receded from her muscles, the anger had faded from her mind. She rose, turned off the music and walked outside onto the patio.

The nights were cool now, the air crisp. She gazed out at the dark sky, let her mind and her heart open to the night. To night thoughts. To—

Like a comet flashing across the sky, the thought came to her, and she knew. The link between Richard and Down Home Foods was as clear as crystal. Tomorrow, she'd wrap up the case.

And she'd do it on her own.

12

SAM SPENT the rest of the evening planning. If she was going to prove herself to Wade, she had to think about her strategy carefully. She'd do nothing reckless, nothing impulsive; she'd plan for every eventuality. Finally satisfied, she went to bed.

Her alarm woke her early. "This is the day," she told herself as she hurried to get dressed. The day of reckoning. The day she'd prove her mettle.

She had decided to make her preliminary arrangements by phone. Watching the clock, she ate a quick breakfast, then made two calls. Afterward, she slipped on a jacket and went out into the cool November morning. She'd left so early that almost no traffic clogged the streets, so she made good time. In less than an hour, she pulled into the parking lot at Down Home Foods.

She waited in her office until nine, then took the elevator up. She went to the last office in the hall, knocked and waited. In a moment, the door opened.

Keith Nelson's eyes widened. "Sam, what are you doing here?"

"I came to talk to you." Without waiting to be invited inside, she stepped into his office. She glanced quickly at his hand as she walked past him. Yes, she'd been right. She turned and stood by the desk, waiting for him.

Looking puzzled, Keith followed her. "What about?"

"Have you heard that Richard Merchant was arrested yesterday?"

Keith's expression gave nothing away. He sat in the desk chair. "No, why would I have heard that? I'm sorry to hear it, of course, but I hardly know Richard."

"Weren't you fraternity brothers in college?"

Keith swallowed. "I..."

"At the University of Arizona," she prodded.

Keith's smile seemed a bit forced. "Um, now that you mention it, I guess we were. He was a couple of years behind me so I must have forgotten. If I can do anything for Richard, well, of course I'll be happy to. Is that why you came to talk to me?"

"No, and I think you've done quite a bit for Richard already."

"What do you—"

"You stole Down Home's new chili recipe and gave it to Richard, didn't you?" She walked to Keith and stood before him, hands on her hips. "*Didn't* you?"

Keith gave her the most innocent look she'd seen outside of a baby nursery. "Sam, what are you talking about?"

He was a cool one, she thought . . . unlike his pal Richard. "You know what I'm talking about," she said.

Keith shook his head and stood. "No, I don't. I know the company's planning a new chili, but why would I steal it? Maybe Richard Merchant has reason to want it, but I don't. What would I do with it?"

For a moment, Sam thought she'd made a ghastly mistake. A herd of butterflies began fluttering in her stomach. "I..."

"Honey—" Keith's voice lowered to a silky purr "—where did you get this bizarre idea? Did your boyfriend come up with it? Is it because you rode in with me the other night, because we used to be . . . together?" He took her by the shoulders, holding her gently in place. "Is he jealous?" he murmured and bent his head.

"Stop it, Keith." Sam shoved his arms to the side. Her uncertainty of a moment ago had vanished. Now she was mad. "You asked me what you'd do with the recipe," she said in a soft voice. "Give it to Richard in return for the money to buy a new Porsche, that's my guess. Well, am I right?"

Keith spread his hands. "Of course not." Now he, too, was angry. "And I don't have to take this from you."

"Right. You can talk to my grandfather. With a lawyer present if you like." She swung around, went to the door and opened it. The security guard stood in the hall. "Come in, Stan. You can take Mr. Nelson to Mr. Brewster's office."

When she looked back at Keith, she saw that his face had turned a dull red. "You bitch," he growled. "If you'd married me, I'd have had it all. I wouldn't have needed to—" He caught himself. As the guard took Keith's arm, his voice cracked. "Did Richard . . . ?"

Sam shook her head. "Richard didn't say a thing. I figured it out from your ring and the mug on his desk. Same crest."

She watched as the guard led Keith out of the room, then went back to her office and sat down. For a few moments, she was too drained to move, then the realization that she'd solved the case dawned. She laughed and hugged herself.

She reached for the phone, then changed her mind. What she wanted more than anything was to see the look on Wade's face when she told him. She was entitled to gloat.

SAM HAD NEVER BEEN to Wade's house, but she knew his address. He lived in tree-shaded Southampton, a neighborhood close to the medical center, the Museum District and Rice University. She was surprised to find that the house was a brick-and-glass contemporary with a beautifully landscaped yard. Why that should surprise her, she wasn't sure. Perhaps she'd pictured him living in a garret as he'd once suggested.

She parked in front and went to the door. Wade answered and seemed as surprised to see her as Keith had been. "Sam?" he said.

She grinned at him. "May I come in?"

He took her hand and drew her inside and into his arms. "What a nice surprise to find you on my doorstep."

She'd been hurt and angry yesterday, but this was today, and her lips parted automatically for his kiss. It was long and satisfying. When he drew back, she said, "I came to tell you some news."

He put his arm around her shoulder and guided her across the room. "What?"

"The chili thief is under wraps."

"Richard?"

"No, what you thought a couple of weeks ago was right. Keith Nelson stole it."

"K—" He stopped midstride. "When? How?"

"Oh, Wade, I figured it out last night. This morning, I went to his office and confronted him."

He caught her by the shoulders. "You...you...confronted him? On your own?"

"Yes, I confronted him, and no, not completely on my own. A security guard was outside the door." *And don't spoil it,* she thought. *Please don't.*

"Sam!" He lifted her off the floor and spun her around. "You're wonderful!"

She laughed down at him, the sound triumphant. "It was a piece of cake."

He set her down. "I want to hear all about it, but damn, I have to testify before the grand jury on the McKenzie case in half an hour. Will you wait?"

"Yes."

"I shouldn't be long. Two hours maybe. Make yourself at home. Coffee's made, and you can fix whatever else you want." He took a step toward the door, then turned back. "And, Sam . . ."

"Yes."

"Just this." He kissed her again, long and hard, then hurried off.

Sam spread her arms and twirled around. She felt wonderful. She kicked off her shoes and sauntered through the living room. He'd told her to make herself at home, so she would.

She poured herself a cup of coffee in the sunny kitchen and sipped it at the table. But she couldn't miss the chance to see where and how Wade lived, so she set the cup down and strolled through the other rooms.

She glanced into the master bedroom with its king-size bed covered with a quilt in shades of brown and tan, but she decided she'd wait to explore that room with Wade.

To the left, she saw a small room, lined with bookshelves. A laptop computer with a stack of papers beside it sat on a wide oak desk. His office.

Slowly, Sam took a step inside, then another. She examined the shelves, crammed with mysteries, classics, history books. One shelf was devoted to books on the craft of writing, others to books he must use in his research—volumes on poisons, weapons, crime investigation. And there were his own books, lined up on the shelf above his desk along with the Edgar award he'd received from Mystery Writers of America. As much as they'd talked about his writing, now for the first time, she truly absorbed the fact that Wade was Nick Petrelli's creator.

She ran her fingers over the ceramic statue of Edgar Allan Poe, glanced at a book lying open on the desk—*Corporate Espionage*—then at the papers between it and the computer. *The Pet Food Pirate: A Nick Petrelli Mystery.* His manuscript.

She'd been wanting to read it. She sat at his desk, turned over the title page, hesitated. "Go ahead," she told herself. The last time they'd talked about it, he'd said, "Yeah, maybe." She picked up the first page.

Instantly, she was absorbed in Nick Petrelli's world, as the CEO of Canine Meals called Nick in because the formula for a new dog biscuit was missing.

On page two, Allison McGuire appeared. Wade had been honest. No one would connect Allison with Sam. She was much more like Tonya—a saucy brunette psychologist who headed up the firm's personnel division. The only similarities between Al and Sam were their masculine nicknames and the fact that they were helping the detective solve the mystery.

Still, she had to keep in mind that Wade's characters were based on real life, especially Nick. Nick was Wade's alter ego. What Nick did or thought must surely be a reflection of Wade. She continued reading.

In chapter four, Nick and Al had their first love scene. Sam had been expecting it. Nick was, after all, a lover *extraordinaire* and he always got involved with a woman in the story. Sam's cheeks heated as she read the scene in which Nick made love to Al on the floor of Randall Porter's office. She remembered all too clearly lying next to Wade behind the couch in Helen's office and Wade's evident arousal. So Nick had taken that spark to its natural conclusion.

Sam checked her watch. Another hour before Wade should return. She read further.

In chapter eight, she came upon a second love scene, this one at Al's condo. It was clear by now that Al had fallen for Nick. Most of the female characters in Wade's books did. Nick, she knew, never returned those feelings. Like Wade, Nick liked women, but he didn't fall in love.

Wade certainly did know how to write a love scene. Sam felt her pulse speed up as she read. Afterward, Nick and Al fell asleep, but in the middle of the night Nick awoke.

Nick lay in Al's bed, her body wrapped around his. When he started to get up, she caught his arm. "Stay the night."

Nick shook his head. He never stayed all night with a woman, no matter how great the sex. He turned away.

She stroked his back. "I need you, Nick."

"Don't," he said. "Don't get any ideas. What's between us—it's a short-term thing."

Sam laid the sheet down. Pain surged through her. Al McGuire might not be her, but Nick Petrelli was definitely Wade. She could even hear Wade's voice as Nick spoke to Al.

Sam continued to read. On the next page, Nick was outside, getting into his pickup.

His thoughts turned to the calf sired by his prize bull and born the day before.

"Rat!" Sam mumbled. Not two minutes had passed and Nick had already forgotten Al. She'd been replaced in his mind by a cow!

Wade had said he didn't believe in long-term commitments. But somehow, seeing his philosophy in black and white, seeing his characters—Nick especially—play it out with all the emotion Wade could evoke made his statement all the more real, all the more hurtful.

Sam felt a tear slide down her cheek. A tear? Samantha Brewster didn't shed tears. Never! She got angry, but she never cried. At least she hadn't until she'd met Wade Phillips.

She trudged out of his office and back down the hall to the living room. She'd felt bad enough when Keith had implied he'd wanted to marry her so he could "have it all." Keith wasn't important to her, never had been, really.

But Wade! Wade had told her *in print* that she was just a fling, a limited-time bed partner, nothing more. *Nick speaks for me*, he'd told her once. Well, he'd spoken, loud and clear.

Sam glanced down and saw that she'd taken her handkerchief out of her pocket and had begun twisting it viciously. Too bad she didn't have Wade's neck between her fingers.

Damned if she'd stay and wait for him. She went into the kitchen, found a notepad and scribbled on it. She propped the sheet of paper against the phone and left his house. He could find another lover. Her term was over.

And so was his.

WADE WHISTLED as he drove home. Don Juanito was pretty sure to be indicted. Nick's latest story was finished and ready to be expressed to his editor. Harold could celebrate tonight at Lutece. He'd be getting his percentage of a fat advance check shortly.

And the chili case was solved. He couldn't believe Sam had wrapped it up herself. She really did have the makings of a top-notch detective. He'd begun to realize it after he left her yesterday, and last night as he lay in bed wishing she was in his arms, he'd known it with a certainty he couldn't deny. She'd been correct yesterday; he knew that, too. He had no right to interfere with her dreams, no more business than Marlene had had to meddle with his.

He knew some other things, too, he thought as he turned into his driveway. And he could hardly wait to tell Sam about them. He parked and hurried across the yard to the front door.

The living room was empty.

"Sam," he called. No answer.

He checked the back patio, the bedrooms, his office. She'd gone. But why?

In the kitchen he found her note:

Dear Wade,
The case is finished. Our relationship is, too. Don't bother to call.

　　　　　　　　　　　　　　　　　　Samantha

"What the hell!" He sank onto the chair and read the terse note again. Had the world suddenly gone mad? Had Samantha? What in God's name had happened in the past two hours to change her from a glowing, happy woman to someone who would write the cold, clipped message he held in his hand?

He dropped his head into his hands. Not three weeks ago, he'd have ended their relationship with little more than mild regret. Not now. Now he wanted to make it long-term. Forever. He wanted love, marriage, a houseful of little P.I.s.

Damn, he hurt. Bad enough to have broken ribs tormenting you every time you breathed or moved. Now he ached *inside* his chest. Right where his heart lay.

He grabbed the phone and called her office. "I'm sorry. Ms. Brewster is out for the day," the receptionist said.

He tried her house, her grandparents', even Tonya's. No one knew where she was. Okay, he wasn't a private investigator for nothing. He'd find her. Within an hour, he'd track her down.

THE NEXT MORNING, Sam plodded across the Down Home parking lot. The glorious morning sunshine mocked her mood. She felt as if she were wading against a strong current. After leaving Wade's yesterday, she'd driven to Galveston, walked the beach for hours, then found a hotel room where she'd sat and stared out the window. She couldn't remember hurting this much, but then, she couldn't remember caring this much about someone.

It was over. *Look ahead. Think of the future. Time heals everything.* Platitudes.

But she didn't have much choice. Life went on, and she'd have to cope. She could go back to Dallas, open an office there where she wouldn't be likely to run into Wade. One thing she wouldn't do anymore was cry. She'd used up all her tears yesterday.

She nodded a good-morning to the security guard and took the elevator to her floor. She'd left Galveston before sunup. Most of the offices were still empty. Maybe she could get some work done. She opened her office door.

"Good morning." Wade rose from her chair and started toward her.

Sam took a step back. "Get out of here."

"Not until we talk." He caught her arm.

Futilely, Sam tried to twist away. She reached toward the desk. "I'm calling security."

"I don't think so."

Sam's eyes narrowed. She grabbed Wade's wrist, gave it a jerk and knocked him flat.

"Lord, Sam!" he croaked. "My ribs."

She stood over him, hands on her hips. "You bastard," she said in a calm, controlled voice.

"Wh-what did . . . I do?"

"I read your book."

He blinked once, then again. "You read . . . You *what?*" he roared.

"You heard me. I read—"

He tried to get up but sagged back on the floor with a moan. "Hell with it," he muttered. "I can yell at you just as well flat on my back. Who gave you permission?" he bellowed.

"You did."

"Never."

"We talked on the way to Terlingua. You said—"

"I said maybe. Maybe means *maybe*." He shut his eyes. "Damn it, Samantha, having you read my personal stuff— that hurts."

"We're even then. Reading it hurt me, too."

Wade opened one eye. "You may as well tell me what you read that made you deck me. Then I can leave and die in peace."

"'Don't get any ideas,'" she mimicked. "'What's between us—it's a short-term thing.'"

"Jeez, Sam. Nick said that. I didn't."

Her fists clenched. "You *are* Nick."

He put an arm over his eyes, then moved it away and squinted at her. "How far did you read?"

"Chapter eight, page one fifty-three." She reached for the phone. "Now you know. You can get out."

His hand shot out and grabbed her ankle. He yanked, and she toppled over, sprawling across his legs. He sucked in his breath, struggled to a sitting position and held her down across his lap. "I'm not going anywhere until we talk."

She tightened her lips and glowered up at him.

"Why did Nick's conversation matter to you?" When she didn't respond, he gave her a little shake. "Answer me, Sam. Please."

"Oh, why not? I've already made a fool of myself. A little

more won't hurt." She took a breath. "Because I care about you."

"I care about you, too," he said.

"Me and the cows."

He let out a curse. "I don't have any cows. And don't tell me Nick does. That's beside the point."

She stared at him for a moment, then said, "Why are you so angry that I read the book?"

"Trust. If I'd handed it to you and said, 'Read it'—and I probably would have soon—that would be one thing. Having you pick it up is another."

She hadn't thought of that. "I'm sorry. I would never have read the book without your permission. I really thought you meant yes." She looked away.

He put a finger under her chin and forced her gaze back to his. "Why didn't you read the rest?"

"You told me before that Nick speaks for you. I'd read enough."

He shook his head. "No, you didn't. During the story, Nick changes. He begins to see that . . . Wait a minute. I have the disk in my car." He eased her off his lap. "Will you wait here and let me show you, or do I have to hog-tie you?"

Sam stuck out her chin. "I'll wait."

Wade pulled himself slowly to his feet and left her office. Five minutes later, he returned, disk in hand. He inserted it in Sam's computer, called up a file and paged through it. "This is the last chapter. Read."

Sam took his place in front of the computer. She read:

Nick opened the door. Al stood on the threshold, suit-case in hand. "You asked me to move in with you. Here I am."

"Not good enough," Nick said. He took the suitcase and set it down inside the door, then swept Al up in his arms. "Let's make it legal, babe."

"You mean . . . ?"

"Yeah, tie the knot."

Eyes wide, Sam turned to look at Wade. He put his hands on her shoulders. "That's what Nick Petrelli says—he's a pretty plainspoken guy. Let me sit down, and I'll show you what Wade Phillips says." He took her place at the desk, opened a new file and began to type:

I love you, Samantha. More than I ever thought possible. I want to spend the rest of my life with you.

He swung around and reached for her hands. "That's what *I* say."

"Oh, Wade." Sam sighed as he pulled her down into his lap. "I want to say yes. I love you, too. But I have to live my life the way I choose."

"There's more." Reaching around her, he typed:

I won't stand in the way of your dreams. In fact, I support them. How about a business partnership, too?

"Do you mean it?" Sam asked.

"Yes. I realize I was being selfish in trying to deny you what you want most. You're too good at it to do anything else."

Touched beyond measure, Sam could say nothing. She could only look at him and smile.

"Kiss me," Wade murmured. "Then you write the ending."

Their mouths met in a kiss of love and joy. When they broke apart, Sam turned back to the keyboard.

"Yes," she said. "I'll be your life partner in love *and* business."

And they lived happily ever after.

Weddings by DeWilde

*Since the turn of the century the elegant and
fashionable DeWilde stores have helped brides
around the world turn the fantasy of their "Special
Day" into reality. But now the store and three
generations of family are torn apart by the divorce of
Grace and Jeffrey DeWilde. As family members face
new challenges and loves—and a long-secret
mystery—the lives of Grace and Jeffrey intermingle
with store employees, friends and relatives in this
fast-paced, glamorous, internationally set series. For
weddings and romance, glamour and fun-filled
entertainment, enter the world of DeWilde . . .*

*Twelve remarkable books, coming to you
once a month, beginning in April 1996*

Weddings by DeWilde begins with
Shattered Vows
by Jasmine Cresswell

Here's a preview!

"SPEND THE NIGHT with me, Lianne."

No softening lies, no beguiling promises, just the curt offer of a night of sex. She closed her eyes, shutting out temptation. She had never expected to feel this sort of relentless drive for sexual fulfillment, so she had no mechanisms in place for coping with it. "No." The one-word denial was all she could manage to articulate.

His grip on her arms tightened as if he might refuse to accept her answer. Shockingly, she wished for a split second that he would ignore her rejection and simply bundle her into the car and drive her straight to his flat, refusing to take no for an answer. All the pleasures of mindless sex, with none of the responsibility. For a couple of seconds he neither moved nor spoke. Then he released her, turning abruptly to open the door on the passenger side of his Jaguar. "I'll drive you home," he said, his voice hard and flat. "Get in."

The traffic was heavy, and the rain started again as an annoying drizzle that distorted depth perception made driving difficult, but Lianne didn't fool herself that the silence inside the car was caused by the driving conditions. The air around them crackled and sparked with their thwarted desire. Her body was still on fire. Why didn't Gabe say something? she thought, feeling aggrieved.

Perhaps because he was finding it as difficult as she was to think of something appropriate to say. He was thirty

years old, long past the stage of needing to bed a woman just
so he could record another sexual conquest in his little black
book. He'd spent five months dating Julia, which suggested he was a man who valued friendship as an element in
his relationships with women. Since he didn't seem to like
her very much, he was probably as embarrassed as she was
by the stupid, inexplicable intensity of their physical response to each other.

"Maybe we should just set aside a weekend to have wild,
uninterrupted sex," she said, thinking aloud. "Maybe that
way we'd get whatever it is we feel for each other out of our
systems and be able to move on with the rest of our lives."

His mouth quirked into a rueful smile. "Isn't that supposed to be my line?"

"Why? Because you're the man? Are you sexist enough
to believe that women don't have sexual urges? I'm just as
aware of what's going on between us as you are, Gabe. Am
I supposed to pretend I haven't noticed that we practically
ignite whenever we touch? And that we have nothing much
in common except mutual lust—and a good friend we be-
trayed?"

Cindy Reed of Houston, Texas, made history by winning her
second consecutive championship title at the
1993 CASI Terlingua International Chili Championship.
This is her history-making recipe:

"Cin-Chili" Chili

STEP 1:

2 lbs	beef chuck tender cut into 3/8" cubes
1 tsp	cooking oil
1 tbsp	dark chili powder
2 tsp	garlic (granulated)

In a three-quart heavy saucepan, add the above ingredients while
browning the meat.

STEP 2:

1 8oz can	tomato sauce
1 14 1/2 oz can	beef broth
1 tsp	chicken bouillon granules
1 tsp	jalapeno powder
1 tbsp	onion powder
2 tsp	garlic powder
1/2 tsp	red pepper
1 tsp	white pepper
1 pint	spring water
1 tbsp	dark chili powder
2	serrano peppers
1/2 tsp	salt

Combine seasonings and add to beef mixture. Bring to a boil,
reduce heat and simmer for 1 1/2 hours. Float 2 serrano peppers.

STEP 3:

1 tbsp	paprika
1 pkg	sazon seasoning (MSG)
1 tsp	onion powder
1 tsp	garlic powder
1/2 tsp	white pepper
5 tbsp	medium and dark chili powders

Combine seasonings and add to beef mixture. Bring to boil, reduce
and simmer for 20 minutes. You may add water or beef broth for
consistency. Remove serrano peppers when they become soft.

STEP 4:

2 tsp	cumin
1/8 tsp	salt

Add above ingredients and simmer for 10 minutes.

Bestselling authors

ELAINE
COFFMAN
RUTH LANGAN

and

MARY McBRIDE

Together in one fabulous collection!

OUTLAW
Brides

Available in June wherever Harlequin
books are sold.

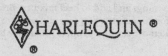

HARLEQUIN ®

Women throughout time have
lost their hearts to:

Starting in January 1996, Harlequin Temptation
will introduce you to five irresistible, sexy rogues.
Rogues who have carved out their place in history,
but whose true destinies lie in the arms of
contemporary women.

#569 *The Cowboy,* Kristine Rolofson
(January 1996)

#577 *The Pirate,* Kate Hoffmann
(March 1996)

#585 *The Outlaw,* JoAnn Ross
(May 1996)

#593 *The Knight,* Sandy Steen
(July 1996)

#601 *The Highwayman,* Madeline Harper
(September 1996)

Dangerous to love, impossible to resist!

RAC

THE WRONG BED

The Wrong Bed! The Wrong Man!
The Ultimate Disaster!

Christina Cavanaugh was *supposed* to be on her
honeymoon. Except the wedding got temporarily
canceled, their flight was delayed while the luggage
went to Europe—and the bridal suite was flooded!

Hours later a frazzled, confused Christina crept into
her fiancé's bed. But it was the wrong bed...
containing the wrong man. And when she
discovered the shocking truth it was too late!

Enjoy honeymoon bedlam and bliss in:

#587 HONEYMOON WITH A STRANGER
by Janice Kaiser

Available in May wherever Harlequin books are sold.

HARLEQUIN®

Temptation

BRIDE'S BAY RESORT

UNLOCK THE DOOR TO GREAT ROMANCE AT BRIDE'S BAY RESORT

Join Harlequin's new across-the-lines series, set in an exclusive hotel on an island off the coast of South Carolina.

Seven of your favorite authors will bring you exciting stories about fascinating heroes and heroines discovering love at Bride's Bay Resort.

Look for these fabulous stories coming to a store near you beginning in January 1996.

Harlequin American Romance #613 in January
Matchmaking Baby by Cathy Gillen Thacker

Harlequin Presents #1794 in February
Indiscretions by Robyn Donald

Harlequin Intrigue #362 in March
Love and Lies by Dawn Stewardson

Harlequin Romance #3404 in April
Make Believe Engagement by Day Leclaire

Harlequin Temptation #588 in May
Stranger in the Night by Roseanne Williams

Harlequin Superromance #695 in June
Married to a Stranger by Connie Bennett

Harlequin Historicals #324 in July
Dulcie's Gift by Ruth Langan

Visit Bride's Bay Resort each month wherever Harlequin books are sold.

HARLEQUIN®

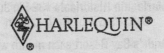

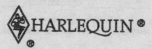

HARLEQUIN®